ON
EARTH
BENEATH
SKY

Also by Chath pierSath

After: Poems
Sinat and the Instrument of the Heart
This Body Mystery: Poems and Paintings

Anthologies in which he is represented:

Children of Cambodia's Killing Fields: Memoirs by Survivors
Prayers for a Thousand Years: Blessings and Expressions of Hope
    for the New Millennium
The Merrimack Literary Review
Where the Road Begins
River Muse: Tales of Lowell and the Merrimack Valley
Atlantic Currents: Connecting Cork and Lowell

ON EARTH BENEATH SKY

Poems and Sketches

Chath pierSath

LP

Loom Press
Lowell & Amesbury
Massachusetts
2020

Loom Press, P.O. Box 1394, Lowell, MA 01853 & 15 Atlantic View, Amesbury, MA 01913
www.loompress.com • info@loompress.com (To contact the author or order copies)

Cover paintings: Chath pierSath
Design: Joseph Marion, marionnyc.com
Printing: King Printing Co., Inc., Lowell, MA

Text set in Roboto & Crimson

For Dr. Charles Nikitopoulos

Contents

CLAIM ME, AMERICA

I LOST MY KAMPUCHEA

MOTHER, I'M COMING HOME

BODY & SOUL

PARIS

EPILOGUE

Introduction

Thank you for reading my book.

I was born Uy Buon Tern in Cambodia in 1970. I came to the United States in 1981 with the name Thouen Bou (known in high school as T-Bo) as a refugee, a survivor of the Khmer Rouge genocide in which political fanatics killed millions of innocent people in my home country. Alongside American soldiers in the Vietnam War, my father fought against the Vietcong, the guerrilla forces opposing the armies of the United States and South Vietnam. He was killed in a battle against the Vietcong when I was two years old.

The Khmer Rouge seized power in Cambodia when I was five. In three years, eight months, and twenty days under their rule, the Khmer Rouge turned the country into Year Zero, full of "Killing Fields" and torture prisons. Their goal was to make a new agrarian society, copying the Maoist Cultural Revolution in China. There, as in Cambodia, vast numbers of people were driven out of their cities and villages to work in the rice fields and dig irrigation canals. During this time, I was not allowed to attend school. Along with other children my age, I was put to work in a labor camp and given little or nothing to eat.

By 1979, with the Americans out of Vietnam, the Vietcong invaded Cambodia and drove the Khmer Rouge into the frontier. My family was freed to search for separated members. We returned to our home village, where my oldest brother was smuggling people out of Cambodia into a refugee camp on the Thai-Cambodian border. That's how I fled. My brother took his wife first, and then he came for my second-oldest sister and me. We lived in the camp for one year before our application to settle in the United States was accepted and processed.

The U.S. adopted, raised, and educated me. In America, I was able to attend school for the first time. I became literate in English instead of Khmer, my maternal tongue. I can speak Khmer, but I cannot read and write the language. I lived first in Boulder and then Denver, Colorado, until I completed high school.

My American education provided the historical, social, and cultural contexts in which I learned to understand life as a journey. In the sixth grade, I became comfortable using English. I read as many books as possible and memorized as many words from the dictionary that I thought I could use. I had a teacher and a homeroom of classmates and friends. I was pulled out of class every day for special help in reading and writing, one-on-one tutoring with someone who was patient and kind. She taught me sounds and rhymes. We read fairy tales and played word games.

Before landing in America, I was not aware of this country or any others beyond neighboring Laos, Thailand, and Vietnam. I grew up in a small rural village near the Thai-Cambodian border. I hadn't seen planes or cars. I hadn't been in a home or an apartment with indoor plumbing. I hadn't been on an escalator or elevator. The toilet in an airplane scared me the first time I used it because of the loud, sucking sound it made when flushed. Cities, airports, cars, and moving things, objects and billboards mesmerized me when I rode in a car. Boulder was clean and full of big beautiful houses. There were mountains and forests where I roamed looking for wild fruit and berries like I did back in Cambodia.

Life as a newcomer wasn't easy because we started from scratch, working toward the American Dream of a better neighborhood, acceptance, and a home of our own. My brother and his wife worked in a ribbon factory seven days a week to save money and buy a house. After the security of a friendly homeroom in the sixth grade, my school experience went downhill. Bullying by other children made me fearful and insecure, but I adapted and got through the trouble.

Whenever I felt sad, nervous, or angry, I thought of the experience I had left behind in Cambodia. My U.S. situation was better than war, better than slaving in the labor camp with nothing to eat. No matter how poor, we could afford to eat. My mother died during the ongoing Khmer Rouge incursions and poverty that war had rendered. She fell ill and passed when I was twelve years old in America.

When I turned eighteen, I studied and took my citizenship test and became a naturalized American citizen. I changed my name to Chath pierSath, which means the temple of the nation. I graduated from World College West, in Petaluma, California. I then moved to San Francisco for a year before returning to Cambodia to work as a volunteer in the human rights field in 1994.

When I returned to Cambodia for the first time in thirteen years, I reunited with some of my family members: an older brother and two sisters and an uncle whom I met for the first time. One older brother had died of AIDS, which I write about in this book ("Kampuchea").

I returned to America in 1996 and lived in Lowell, Massachusetts, for seven years. This was when I started to read the work of Jack Kerouac and understand the city through the prism of his life experience and spirituality. Lowell has the second-largest Cambodian community outside of Cambodia, only Long Beach in Southern California has more Cambodians and Cambodian Americans. Today in Lowell, sixty-one percent of Cambodians are foreign-born while thirty-nine percent are U.S. citizens by birth.

While working full time in the city, I would paint and write before and after work, inspired by poets and other writers and painters I had read about and the lives they had lived. I tried to live my own life, as free as Walt Whitman, by jotting down memories, celebrating my own body electric, journaling, documenting, reflecting on the road—the journey, all the sorrow and pain of a life and the world, the nostalgia for home and country, the people I met, what their lives would and could have been, the poverty and riches of man, the war and violence within nature, the wars and conflicts we fight, the battle for survival, the joy and sadness of life, its loneliness—my loneliness, laying down its own leaves of grass, the beautiful and ugly all in view, all within reach as other writers have paved the way, both to human torment and despair as well as to joy and human resilience.

Now, I live between countries as a native and adopted son. I travel the world to learn about and be in new cultures like I had done when I first arrived in the mountains of Colorado. History and people fascinate me. Visiting other places around the world, I learn about myself and what it's like to be a free global citizen.

I am the son of two countries. I know Cambodia by birth and America by the life I've lived, by the books I've read. In English, I channel my understanding of human expression. I write this way, from the vegetable-and-fruit farm in Bolton, Massachusetts, where I live, and sometimes from Paris or Phnom Penh. I write while torn by confusion about where home is, the risk of stagnation, and the danger of being a body in stasis, writing with a mind in constant grief and a heart often too heavy to carry around.

—Chath pierSath

MY MOTHER WANTED
MY BROTHER
TO TAKE ME
BACK   TO   HER

No. I can't risk your life and mine a third time.
The jungle is thick with mines and Thai pirates.
What is she thinking?
We're going to America.

America, I said.
Does America have rivers I can swim in?
Will there be rice fields to roam and trees to climb?
Will there be fish to catch?

America has everything and more—school, your future, he said.
I'll go with you then.
I'll return when it's safe, &
After I've learned something to make her proud of me.

Now, my brother explained,
Once we get on that bus, you won't be able to see her for a while.
I can still send you back with a friend.
No, I want to go to America with you, I said.

She won't know I got on the bus.
She won't think of me in a place she hasn't seen.
She won't miss me at the border she refused to cross.
The farther away I am, the closer she'll be to me.

Once I got on the bus,
Time sped past my goodbyes.
The bus was that time without my mother
Unlike my time on a train with her.

She took care of me,
So now I had to take care of myself.
From a bus and into a plane.
The route back to her was thick with puffy clouds.
I thought—I won't see her again.

CLAIM ME, AMERICA

Un Réfugié

My brother spoke French, *Un Réfugié*.
He carried the IOM bag with our tags.
Refugees across borders,
From camp to Bangkok, on a plane to Manila.
Refugee route. Which bus to take, airport to airport?
We met faces unlike ours, children begging, pulling pockets.

All refugees sat silently in a bus,
Thinking and fearing what we saw,
Watching for the green highlands of Bataan.
It was fun being a refugee—run and play,
Swim beneath a waterfall, pick wild mangoes,
& bananas. Like home, the monsoon felt like home.

After six months, on another bus to an airport,
Then onto a giant Pan Am plane to San Francisco,
And then another bus to be quarantined in army barracks
To learn how to floss and brush my teeth.

Doctor checked eyes and ears,
Reflexes, knocking on knees and elbows.
X-ray showed TB in the lungs. Pills prescribed.
Vaccination for mumps, polio, and measles.
Welcome to America, he said.

One more plane to Denver's glittery Stapleton Airport.
So many different people in beautiful garb, wearing shoes,
Women in high heels tap, tap, tap the shiny floor.
An aunt and husband waited for us with coats and proper shoes.
In their car I sat in back, staring at things speeding by,
Trying to catch up to what I was seeing, trembling,

Teeth chattering, controlling the urge to vomit,
Thinking, If my mother was here, I could hold her hand.

My first day of school, onto the bus with a backpack of books.
I always sat by the window, face against the clear glass,
Watching trees chase me & cumulonimbus clouds pass,
Sun leaving the rice field behind.

Without English, I watched other kids play.
I learned the word refugee.
From a small black and white TV, learned to be American.
Channel surfing by hand, clicking the knob.
Shivering in thick blankets, slow to warm.

An infant learning to walk and talk the new tongue.
Reciting a strange alphabet and all the words that pertained to me.
Refugee, exile, country-less child, stateless body,
Speechless ward of the court,
Nesting in the mountains of Boulder, Colorado.
Refugee, a temporary resident alien.

America, My America

Indebted to you, America,
My eyes aren't enough, for I have seen freedom.
My heart you can take
For I have felt hatred and war.
My gratitude in every limb born to you and for you,
Perhaps is all I have to give.
Take my ears for I've heard the Liberty Bell from Mount Rushmore.
Mark me a donor. Take my spleen, kidneys, and lungs.
My privileged American life can take my eyes, after all.
My arms and legs, I am willing to sacrifice.
Let me die for freedom and democracy,
For peace and prosperity, justice and liberty for all.
I salute you, America, for helping my dream take flight,
Letting me be, see and become, to work and play,
Eat and sleep to life's breathlessly beautiful hills,
Mountains, valleys, above and below.
This land is your land . . . this land is my land,
Field to field, from California to the New York Island,
Wheat and rye, Iowan corn, grassland,
Native sacred paradise,
On earth and beyond the sky,
Galaxy, and beyond every universe man must explore,
Stars and planets near and far.
To every free spirit, may American-born freedom roar,
Echoing far and wide until all
Tyranny be gone, like doubts and fears,
Gone from the ears I have given America.
From the eyes that witnessed human cruelty,
From the heart that felt freedom, the highway
Paved for kings and queens, the magician
Who appears and disappears by his own magic,

I give all of me, the entirety.

Claim me, America,
A sacrifice worth more than the life I knew before.

Ode to an American Bed

Every night, by twelve, you and me, to silent dreams sweeping the floor, painting the stars, falling to empty wishes and yearnings. Kissing lips and body to warm my flesh. You wait for lights out to take my weight, cushion my back, and absorb my pain and sorrow, send me to warm dreams or horrid nightmares or dreams in the Milky Way. I enter to be cuddled under the goose-feathered duvet.

In December's snow, our room chilled to ice but insulated what it contained, like an igloo—my body warmed enough to toast bread and boil water for tea, my thoughts far, like an open book about distant countries, Sahara dunes, treasure caves, and island castles inhabited by fairies, the smallest people made large by the paradise they tend. I, your king, must think into the future, must close my eyes to visions of a life without war, without borders or countries to conquer and defend against. I must plant flowers, make all people feel beautiful and happy, one planet, one family.

What sea-traveler's adventures have you kept from me? You cannot live without me nor I without you, my security and companion. What rise and fall, tender grief sent eastward for final cremation? What tears could I have shed? What tosses and turns? How restless is the ravishing fire, exquisite flame tongue of dragon spit, muted by the gold color that sparks into flower.

Grant me eternal peace. Let me sleep past dawn while the sun heats my body. Knock down my kingdom. Let my people eat well. Let them drink the clearest, cleanest water. Let them sing and dance, forever free from harm. Grant them the riches of pearls and gemstones from the caves of life and give them knowledge to manage their desire, greed, hunger, and thirst, and give them this bed as you have given me.

Gift of comfort,
Gift of sleep,
Gift of dream,
Safety, and freedom.
America, bed me in your liberty flame.

In Paradise

Among pines and oaks,
An ant under rotten leaves,
In peace, but regret rising in my throat.
Bird chirps and cheers,
Cawing crows mourning friends,
Singing their pecking songs,
Caught up in foolish wars over food and territory.

I can't help but envy their freedom,
How lavish their colorful plumes, sky rulers,
While I farm in the sun, longing for love.
I should live other lives I haven't tried,
Travel as a vagabond, meeting singers and dancers.

Instead, I regress, fantasize, dodge truth, craft false hopes,
Give away my time, my breath, to earn half a life,
Stuck in the now, with tomorrow a last resort.
Waking can be unbearable, aching bones,
Crazy-cursing this serenity, this life, the birds even.
I want someone to squeeze me hard so I can die.
I am all worked up in paradise.

The Loneliest Winter

Doubts pencil-mark my American landscape.
When the lights of the universe go out,
Voices from the past urge me to remove the shawl,
Lie bare, and close my eyes to harsh dreams.
I want to leave you for the indifferent East,
Sun burning the sky, where no eyes turn from hate.
In my humid ancestral home, rice fields become house lots.
Mass graves are buried over to cover the past.

In that capital of scoundrels and dogs,
Bitches are whoring for American dollars to build
Private gilded spires, palaces and pagodas,
Where I was beaten and defeated time again and again,
Yet, I feed on old memories, scents and childhood,
Umbilical ties mocking me for betraying my roots,
Where I feel obligated to serve.

Am I the American West,
Harnessed by the power of electricity
And steam locomotion?
Where my dreams and flight path are birthed?
My wings grow in books and imagination,
Through peace and security in life and work,
Under the roof from which I cannot stray.
I can stand the loneliness of the West,
But not those nights alone in a rat-infested cell of the East,
Where the dead moan and porno-sex groans online,
Where power brokers split haves from have nots
In a country fresh out of hell, and now cloning
A second hell of high fashion, luxe SUVs, and sky-rises.

An American Sex Education

1.
No one was there to tell you the good from the bad,
The right from wrong, but it was time, time to be on your own,
So, you learned by flipping pages of your brother's *Penthouse* spreads—
Nude words manifested, buzzing pollinators with flies open.
Scrambled Playboy channel, the moan arousing.
Is it pain or pleasure? A proclamation, yes!
Constitutional affirmation of an American erection.

Boys and sex explained in puberty, where to touch and see.
Browsing bookstore secretly.
The doctor-author thumbed-up masturbation.
Thighs and muscles, testicles of private moss.
Shifting, your hand-filled heat pumping.
Pornography, geography, geometry,
Road construction, shifting roads, physical destiny,
Rivers and streams, sun, stars, and moon.

What howling beast does not yearn for pleasure?
The dark hours of youth, pornography
In abundance, in hiding, often filled with shame and dirt.
Man and woman, each other's yin and yen.
Key to a lock. Unlock the secrets. What is this yearning, this desire?
Open the flowering buds.
Unnatural when man to another,
Lips unbiblical, songs unsung, Puritanical
Godless, and bestial, the thought of him belonged
To a woman and only his to her.
Never a key to a key or lock to a lock.

America screamed shame as you flowered.
Your body opened for the sun.
Your body was cleansed by the rain.
You think you had it all.
What sorrow and pain love had set aside, you rose
To the challenge—in your throat and in your behind,
Men in your future couldn't be brighter.
The best and the worst.
The beautiful and the ugly.
Walt Whitman's Body Electric.
You sang with and to him, you sang to yourself,
To the body, to your soul, all electrified by the thought
Of freedom, of chanting prayers to Hedone, her father Eros
While you pleasured yourself, your life
In the hands of strangers, the textures and colors
Of the male nudes: Michelangelo's *David*
On the palm of your hand, his marble flesh
Rapturous divinity in a church bell that a hunchback rang.
Take you inside. Covet your beauty in the moment.
Without naming names,
He knows the texture—the taste of your tongue.
The subtle heat radiated from your skin.
Every strand of your hair a bamboo shoot
Reaching for the light.
Oh, how you dreamt for the one
You could love.
With each day's rise, America caught your eyes.

2.
Birds wake me in a spring flowering.
They sing in circles, taking storms to sea.
Clearing my eyes, the light fills up my room.

Glory to the sun, my heart is beating.
What life, what gratitude I owe you. May I now be relieved?
Yawn out the restless convulsion of the past,
Reach for the light of a new day.
America is a bounced book to read.
I write to Walt Whitman to be reincarnated as my lover.
I write to Jack Kerouac to get him to come back to Lowell.
I want him to know that we have crossed paths.
I traveled his roads.
I know his Eastern quest for good dharma.
I am a Khmer-born American with almond-shaped eyes.
I am content, I am beautiful, I like my black hair,
My flat nose, my brown, mahogany skin,
My lips creamed by the kisses of American dawns.
My heart throbs to American lovers, close and distant,
As new exotic days or nights.
In the bay of San Francisco, I discovered my sexuality.
I had been to many oceans and seas,
Where men, like seals, sunbathed on warm rocks and sand.
European men were puppies learning how to bark.
In the marshes of Provincetown, I locked eyes with strangers,
All in the nude, we opened our mouths like seagulls.
The perfect sun gave us vitamin D for hard bones.
My American men are on their way to heaven.
Some opened their holy books, biblical and tongues.
I spoke the truth, shameless before their gods,
I deep-throat Shiva and Buddha, Abraham, and even the Lord.
Mormon elder and Catholic priest would undress for my innocence,
Heaving with the rising mist of snow.

American Monsoon

I miss you in April, rain time.
I miss your lips,
Delicate and rouge.
My fingerprint would go over them
With my eyes inside you
Like a sharpened tender blade,
A prick of my own life into yours.
I miss the green flesh of your room,
High up on stilts, thatch concealed,
Your will over mine,
Arresting me in my place,
You filled my emptiness with your scent of roses.
Your bed was unmade by lovers before me.
Now you're mine in this moment in time to unravel.

Fill my throat with thirst.
Honey my lips to yours.
Give me your swallow to stave off hunger.
Lie down to be undressed by my noble hands.
It's a mango shower in the east all over
This land, your America of tongue and cheek.
Father me to sleep with your English poems
Abreast and on your pillow where I shall be an American.
Rain. Let it rain.
I am done crying.
I am no longer afraid of thunder and lightning.
I am here to sing of peace, done grieving of war.
I am here to play—your charade is perfectly fine.
I am here to dance and forget how I had to run.
I ran into the safety of your arms,
The security of your monsoon rain,
Singing America so I can love again.

Winter in America

I drag out of warmth into the field where birds sing.
I do not mind this instead of the heat in Asia.
I do not miss that country of blood.
I see the barbarians fighting with foreign guns and tanks.
They cannot see beyond the horizon
Or what they must learn to get ahead.
It's war and indifference they want.
It's their tribe and class or nothing.
I shall leave them to battle it all out.
Elsewhere, true freedom is in the wind.
I have a single flight I can take.
My wings possess an array of knowledge,
A mental map of today's past and future.
I am a fowl with a tongue that pecks
And picks out the good seeds from the bad.
I know weather like the lines on my claws.
I shall not fear what I can do on my own.
Without a tribe, a social class or a country,
I am free to roam, feet lifted, arm-span wide,
Yes, open, even in darkness I can see.
Cold as it may be, I will fly now.

What's way up there or down here for me, a forest of wolves?
Maybe the wolves aren't so bad.
Would they take me into their pack?
I can run, keep other animals from worst impulses.
I'm afraid I'd be lonely up there, vanished into the stars.
Space would not know the way my pillow knows that I'm there.
Here, I make a dent, breathe loud enough to be heard.
Out there, I'm not even meteorite dust.

American-Based

The batter spits.
Shoves his left foot against the white plate of home.
He makes eye contact with the pitcher.
He tilts down the right edge of his cap
To buckle it tight to each strand of his hair.
It's him against the other team—nine of them, all dressed the same,
All with different numbers, each bat a signature of a man's worth,
Aiming for the same goal: play to win.

Out there,
America shines,
Business as usual,
Subliminal and routine,
CITGO and Dunkin Donuts,
Samuel Adams beer and Coca-Cola, Bank of America and JetBlue.
Foxwoods, National Car Rental,
And New Balance made-in-America shoes.
Dollars are taped to the store walls.
Democracy and free enterprise are fly balls, fouls, and strikes.

A face-shot of a pitcher is paired with each batter on the screen.
Heroes, Red Sox-ers, Bostonians, thirty thousand-plus,
Dots cheering in waves, brilliant flowers swaying below
Hovering light towers, Prudential and joyous,
Prosperity and peace are familiar, comradery of life.
American God watches from above,
Catholic and Puritan, New England and foreign.
Baseball superstition is spit and bubble gum.
The Holy Virgin birthed sons of baseball in Cuba,
Venezuela, the Dominican Republic island.
As far east as the Japanese shore,

Fans worship the American-based game.

On a diamond-shaped infield carpeted with grass,
The man at bat in a well-fitted uniform
Prepares for the pitcher's bullet, ninety-plus-mile-per-hour speed.
More failures than there are hits.
Slow and patient, each batter meditates on the coming ball.
A homerun gets fans up their feet, cheering
For the star-spangled banner wave.
To be an American is to play baseball.
To be Bostonian is to be a Red Sox.

Each player a man of secrets and technique, skills and talent,
Batting for the run, not out to war but for money and fame.
One man will rise above and make history
Amidst a bounty of cheers and joy extending to boys and girls
Singing *Take me out to the ball game. Take me out with the crowd . . .*

Hyphenated Adam

His name is Adam.
He naturalized his name by adding an A before it.
He likes how his new name sounds.
He was sworn in as Adam Nguyen, Vietnamese-Khmer-American.
His unpronounceable last name keeps him connected to the past.

The Khmer Rouge killed his Vietnamese father.
Dam was a boat person.
His life was in death's hands floating on the sea.
His mother whispered, caressing his face with her index finger.
"Buddha, please let my boy live, my little Dam.
Should I die, let him survive."
She starved, her body brine-swallowed.
Adam sees her float when he flies over the ocean.
Bones glinting in the sun remind him to fight for his life.

His American pillows are stitched with nightmares.
American napalm burning coconut trees.
Monks, in a photograph, immolating themselves.
Kim Phuc and her siblings running, napalm melting her skin.
His mother calls him for dinner.
Bombs explode. He runs.
He couldn't forget how he ran even after he had changed his name.
A boat on an open sea.
"Gook, Go home!"
Adam wants to forget, but his last name Nguyen remains,
Unpronounceable by real Americans. Memory alive inside him.
His past sleeps with his new name.
ADAM.

The Willow Road

Gold dawn after rain. Clear sky, heaven to enter.
Each earth day is an evolution and a revolution.
Death and life share one coin. Rebirth and resurrection,
Calm and chaos are in Shiva's hands.

Lights shine at the speed limit. We crawl toward the sky,
The hope and dream from the night before subsides.
Massachusetts, Route 495 North or South—exits I had not taken.
Paths crossed, not crossed. Intersections. Roundabouts.
Towns and cities evocative and familiar.
Kneel, hands up, palm for rain. What beauty have I seen?

Apples and peaches gold and red. What supple lips can I behold?
Paradise, where the stars point the night to love,
Where travelers yearn for American-born freedom.
Root me here. I want to stay in your boundless joy.
Give me a chance that your merciful hands can feel.

Each time we pass Route 62 West called Willow Road,
On a slanted hill to the left is a grass-mowed heart shape
Made by a man with Parkinson's disease for his late wife.
He placed two chairs side by side at the foot of the heart.
In front, there's a footstool for a bottle of wine and two glasses.
The wife is a ghost visiting, sitting with him at her leisure,
Without his pain in the flesh. The husband lingers,
Begging to leave this earthly life to join his soulmate.
His heart is in the grass for every passing driver to see.
At night in a halo of light we picture man and wife
With their wine glasses, and then on the ground, weeping,
They writhe like two snakes entwined in the grass,
Their love in a heart shape on the slanted hill, seen by all.

The Story My Grandmother Cannot Tell

Grandmother mourns her fate,
Trapped in a narrow high-rise apartment
In the Tenderloin of San Francisco.
She looks to her past where there's only pain.
Looks to the future where there isn't much either.
She's home, during peacetime with friends and neighbors,
Gathering legends and memories of things long gone,
Missing her green rice fields before the gold harvest,
Remembering the monsoon dancing to her lullaby.
Salt in her Cambodian rainfall drips to the ground,
Down the canals and streams of her memory.

In her homeland people die every day without justice.
Her people are still at war.
Staged political atrocities made her a witness.
She had a daughter raped by boys with guns pointed to her breasts.
Her husband was taken in the night, tortured and shot
Because he was an old man who wore glasses.
They did the same to intelligent young women,
To children with clean hands and to people who prayed.

Now, in the America she pictured as paradise,
Grandmother sits fenced-in by fear
That one day her children and grandchildren
Will leave her, spitting English in her face,
Their broken Khmer torturing her.
They have become too American,
Too modern to see that she's too old and fragile to respond,
Too slow to react because she forgets.
She cannot change their minds.
She can only hold onto the good in her past

And the hope that someone will come along to hear the bad.

I am the answer to her solitude. I climb the stairs to visit.
Though not her real grandson, we are linked by pain and flight.
Words are not necessary. We understand eyes and silence.

Encircle

Life rises into day, repeating another season—
The cycle on wheels, this time without the pull of gravity.

Weightlessness and the secrets to happiness spawn the acquisition
Of material things and the loss of meaning, blown to the wind.

The amount of rain and the level of snow needed
To keep the earth from drought—repeating habits.

Expectations set too high—then comes the unexpected.
A birth, a disease, a virus—the odds of surviving shrink.

The Ozone depletion a culling of who's to live and who's to die,
Each cleansing rain, a halo rainbow over the mountain.

Earth heaven, earth hell—the levitation power of grief,
Of torment and despair, the salinity of welling eyes.

The moon shows prints of man whose skin can't truly feel its surface.
The insulated suit proves the danger of space travel.

Chaos is churning—and the glory of life, triumphant, each to its own,
Alone into dust, ash to ash, bellowing profanity, encircling in vain.

I LOST
MY
KAMPUCHEA

Kampuchea

The color of dark clay.
His face
His jawbone knife
His forehead skull
His head larger than his body
His starved flesh.

That night he slept under guava trees
On a bamboo bed beneath the stars.
His older brother feared he would infect the children
If he let him in his thatched house.
He died with his eyes open,
The virus spread and pushed his stiff cold feet.
It was silly to be monogamous.
There was no point to quit drinking or smoking
That night he slept under guava trees.

Her long black hair in braids and in bundles.
Rice stalks wind-swept under blue skies.
She weeps in shouts and screams.
Her earth torched ashen. Her forest was raped and pillaged.
Capitalists who sold her land, took her home, breathe easily,
Polluting her water, poisoning her only livelihood.

She cries, hands toward the sky, choking in her own blood.
Mother Earth releases her hair to bring a downpour, but even her hair
Is thirsty, from an ancient tale, her old magic can't change old greed.

I Lost You

I lost you then and now, even today, I've lost you.
Every day, not a day when I had not thought of losing you.
I think I've lost you to the future, too.
I beg and pray, but know I must lose you, the way
A snake sheds its skin, a crab goes soft for another stage of life.

I lost you to the beauty and glory of flowers others desire.
They want you because you're beautiful, fragile, vulnerable.
The repressed lips are voiceless, purple.
Death colors, red and black, death of just king and queen,
That colonial mirror of a faraway place sailing westward,
Taking your breath into exile. Money, power chained you to greed.
Mango sap sealed you shut with your fearful grieving.
You flower what others want, but I cannot smell it even if I try
With good intentions. I can't give you my eyes.

I cannot give my ears, my arms or legs.
The language of the bombers and the colonialists,
Fascist conquerors, insatiable capitalists, and thieves of antiquities
Erased all words I had learned in your umbilical cord.
There's no country on this planet not touched by cruelty.
I am changed, formed and shaped by this consciousness, by blood-
Rivers I floated on and crossed. Innocence gone.

I tried to give what I could, but what I've seen and heard,
Where I had been and what I had done, are nights to your days.
No way to explain in a tongue I don't have,
The sounds and lullabies I've forgotten.
Lost you to the death-stench and skull piles in genocide museums.
I lost you to the dogs eating human feces, who hunt for your soul,
Always hungry, the way I hunger for you.

The rivers and streams sang your name.
Hey, hey, matriarch, beautiful spirit earth,
The ancestral callings you turned to
Gave me no comfort in the language I was not born to speak.
I've lost my country, mother and father.
I've lost the freedom and imagination of a child.
I've lost you today to the bloodthirsty mosquitoes.

War-makers are coming for your bones,
Carrying guns made by robots.
Coming for your trees and water and your burial grounds,
Where every bit of your people will be bought and sold,
And all the rivers will dry as they are dammed for electricity,
All the fish will die,
The drought will even take your tears.

Day of Abandonment

My Prince, your letter folded the American flag. Your Mekong was the color of blood. Your oracle reversed its flow, fated to crumble your kingdom. Shadows were to shape your destiny. An approaching butcher thirsted for your people's blood. He is destined to stop the bullet you loaded and fired.

The Americans left you without a single bomb, grenade-less and bullet-less. Deceived and bitter, with daggering betrayals. On their eagle wings, powered by its gold-studded beak, lies they delivered were classified as foreign aid. Dollars & weapons lent in exchange for valuables. Your miniature kingdom was no longer valued. They left you to the communists, the other imperialist dogs. They left you time, a ticking clock, a cathedral and freak science of locomotion. They left trails of their carpet-bombing, (Vietnam, Laos), your brother American bombers, your father of democracy, liberty and justice. Your giant who runs from David's slings. Their B-52s darkened your blue sky while your people stood with Neutrality signs to welcome their presence. Like the American western buffalo massacred, even the water buffalo died, on its back, legs up, surrendering with shrapnel wounds in the bloody dark mud. Surviving children scrambled for their parents only to find them dead. There were too many bombs to miss an ant.

The green forest, even with the pouring monsoon, burned flat ashen to ground zero. The bombing was a secret of presidential men in suits, bigger, and greater than divine Sihanouk, that debonair prince-turned-king, head of state, brother of yours, had dared to hide the Vietcong beneath his banyan tree of neutrality. Nixon and Kissinger wouldn't have it, so they bombed everything to smithereens. Ambassador John Gunther Dean said he wept with great regret. After all the wars Americans had fought against evil, for democracy and liberty at home and abroad, they abandoned your Cambodia to her own genocide.

One of Gunther Dean's aides sent her last words, a secretary telegraphed her last message. They are here. The gate is open. The Khmer Rouge in black and checkered red-and-white scarves dragged her by the hair and called her a whore of imperialism. Gunther was taken aboard the last helicopter loaded with as many people as he could fit. He walked away with his American flag folded and wrapped in plastic to suffocate its meaning.

"I never believed for a moment," Prince Sirik Matek wrote, *"that you would abandon a people which has chosen liberty. You have refused us your protection and we can do nothing about it. You leave us and it is my wish that you and your country will find happiness under the sky .. .. I have only committed the mistake of believing in you, the Americans."* Bang! The pigeons fled the palace, frightened by your self-defeating death.

That April 12, 1975, that ominous Year of the Rabbit, was lost to revolutionists flapping their red-and-black wings, holding Chinese and Russian guns, looking to spill blood. Gunther's staff members left behind were butchered with their faces to a wall, hands to their heads, bullets sprayed to their backs, execution-style, even infants weren't spared.

Kill one, kill all. Leave no bloodline to take revenge.

Nixon and Kissinger drank tea and coffee, business as usual, in the Oval Office, the shape of a screaming mouth, plotting what nation to abandon next.

Three countries on their own, boarded-up by a new regime, labor camps, re-education camps, torture prisons, and new killing fields. The Pathet Lao out to get CIA corroborators—the Hmong, their women ordered raped, villages razed, every captured man severed and beheaded. Bodily organs of their enemies consumed to strengthen the power to kill, like a hallucinogen, wild for blood, spleens and hearts, boiled or grilled, freshly drawn from men they had taken prisoner. The last American helicopter, a dragonfly, disappeared. Every classified memory in their Embassy went into dark folders.

Red China won. Karl Marx and Lenin won. Pol Pot's now the master, with the power to purge. Lon Nol's soldiers who sided with the Americans, executed. Anyone working for any foreigner, targeted. The educated who can question the Red party, Angkar, tortured and killed. In three years, eight months, and twenty days, to be exact, from the time they took power, from April 17, 1975, to the day the Vietnamese invaded in 1979, the Khmer Rouge sowed their killing fields throughout Cambodia. Bomb craters are ponds visible from a plane. Unexploded ordnance, like sculptures on Easter Island, stick up in rice fields. Cattle that drink water from the bomb-made ponds die. Villagers think that ghosts of the unnamed dead poisoned the water.

You had no friends, no brothers or fathers of liberty. I would not have died by the last bullet they left you. I would have fought to my death, even if I had only a spear, machete, or an axe.

I would have been king before I was a prince. How naïve you were, Your Highness.

Evidence

Framed black-and-white portraits of the bruised and tortured feather-tickled to a smile. Tuol Sleng High School-turned-torture prison. Shackles. Burned men. Charred black skin convulsed upward against the pain of being burned alive, chained to a metal bed spring. The cameraman argued he was trained solely to shoot. Photography for recordkeeping, each body tagged to date and time of arrival, numbered forced confession, the year 1978 showed up the most. Tourists pay an amount to enter the museum and take their selfies, leaving their tuk-tuk drivers outside the barbed-wire enclosure.

Greeting them is one of the eight survivors selling his memoir to make a living. He has shed so many tears in retelling his ordeal that he is dry. Instead, he smiles, shaking hands with strangers, who buy his book like he is a famous novelist after a reading, signing the English version someone translated from Khmer for free. He seems at ease with where he had been tortured, re-seeing everything they did to him, how he was starved and beaten, the voices he heard calling all prisoners traitors and CIA corroborators. A child who could barely speak was as guilty as the mother. As a form of torture, her infant was thrown into the air and bayoneted. The torturers laughed and mocked her as they dragged and beat her.

Another survivor was Van Nath, an artist saved by a lead interrogator to paint Pol Pot's portrait. There's a stone carving of Pot's head someone had marked with a bloody red X. The painter didn't get to paint Pol Pot's face before the Vietnamese marched in as liberators. Instead, he painted scenes of waterboarding, pincer-pulling of nipples, and detaching fingernails and toenails. He never painted himself in any scene, but there's one self-portrait with gray hair, in fear that he would die and take with him everything he had lived through and witnessed. He, too, relived what he went through until he was cried out, and the atrocities normalized by history, accepted as something that just happened, something the guilty still deny in a tribunal. Wealthy countries spend millions to prove that they care about post-genocidal justice.

An hour from the city, most prisoners from here met their executioners in Choeung Ek, The Killing Fields, surrounded by rice fields, from which you see the rising skyscrapers the nouveaux riche construct, a leap forward masking the past with fast money-making enterprises, fueling the same class division as it was before the Khmer Rouge. Greed and authoritarianism framed on the walls of Tuol Sleng, an infant still being breastfed born to a world of nothing, darkness enveloping, the drums of hate scream for blood, the mothers are spat at for claiming a right to feed their children in peace and security, freedom to obtain food and clean water.

The Killing Fields are owned and run by a Japanese company, offering visitors a private tour in his or her mother language. The voice in the earphone points to this and that. Mass grave for children. Mass grave for women without clothes. Further down, the Killing Tree, now full of ribbons covering its bark. Adults and other children tied them in solidarity. The Killing Tree is part of a manicured park now. Mass graves are empty craters without the bones and the skulls.

Garden flowers and shrubs have been brought in. Pathways around a pond and out to the periphery are rice fields where the peasants still plow and sow. The road leading to the death-park mushrooms with modern stylized homes, mahogany wood stilt posts and beams, tiles of shiny clay sparkle on the ground. The Killing Fields bring into the local economy hard dollars to fertilize green landscape with more cycles of blood. Killing caves. Killing Fields. Where Pol Pot once lived and died. His house and his grave attract tourists. Private guards at Ta Mok-the-Butcher's house want five dollars a visit. Bone memorial temple became an urn for an entire people, a nation of charms and cruelty.

This Kampuchea is land and country without toys, but memories of guns and bombs. Tyranny is a way of life. Freedom suppressed. Fear stacks on fear, one man and his family take all the forests, even the palace, the land of the poor, wherever there's enterprise and business opportunity, they take, they sell, and they grab. They sell the city's lakes and tributaries. They sell sand they dredged from the lives of fish and mangrove forest.

A Pol Pot is being weaned and reared for a future dark occasion. Foreign-made weapons are readily available. Eager arms dealers speak many languages. The top leaders have been sentenced to life imprisonment, but they're already old, with only a few years to live. There are still many rogue killers who were reintegrated, who still live among the people, sometimes, survivors know who they are, but they are not being punished. It's like living among serial killers. The work of erasing the memories of those with all the evidence in their hands, their eyes, and their utterances has just begun. Their bodies, full of caution, walk step by step, careful not to trip over the bones and skulls displayed as museum pieces.

The Fallen Era

The day you came home, it poured.
Tears of your children, wailing as news of your death spread.
They thronged to your palace with lotus and incense for you.
Why didn't you live forever?
You were supposed to be divine and immortal.
You were our Father King, the only one we still remember,
The only King who really did anything.
Norodom, don't leave us to the vultures.
These barbarians are selling your Cambodia.
They imprison your heirs and silence them to suffering.
But then, it's better that you left.
You couldn't speak if you wanted to.
All you could do was go to China and sing Karaoke.
What use did you have as an old man?

Now, we miss you in the news,
All the surprises you managed to bring us.
Without you, everything is boring.
The palace is quiet, full of tourists pointing
To where you had lived, where we could never
Find you whenever we needed you.
You preferred your palace in China.
Mao had given you a Carnet de Residence.
I was young then. I called you Father because everybody did.
Now that I am older, I understand why.
You were a star of your own films.
You were a composer of music.
You made Phnom Penh beautiful.
You are the Father of Peace.
You made history because you stood up to the U.S.
You had a vision, and those who stood in your way

Were either killed or imprisoned.
You nursed Kampuchea into modernism.

Then again, that Lon Nol, that evil Pol Pot,
Those damned Khmer Rouge used you.
You couldn't wave your magic wand and make them disappear.
Cambodia had to go through those dark periods
To fulfill a certain prophecy or to learn lessons.
I hope those dark days are over.
Please watch over us. Send us another visionary,
Another King who loves his own people,
Who does not chase foreign women and neglect his duties.
Send us Jayavarman VII. Send us Kala Horm Kong.
Send us another Kem Ley, a hero our children can admire.
Look, we are grieving, missing you.

I am so sorry that I didn't make it to your funeral.
No matter what, you are still my only king.
No one can replace you. I can still hear your voice.
I can't imagine what has been on your mind.
All those years burdened by the politics of man.
You would rather sing and compose music or make movies.
I would not have wanted to be in your shoes.

My Father King

Father King now bronze, a statue, breathing the city's smog.
In bronze suit and shoes, he's on guard, looking at his handiwork,
The park full of Chinese taking photographs of themselves.
A bird on his head, a black dot at rest, drops on his bronze hair.
Up close, His Majesty's metallic face looks like someone else.
The King I knew was small and short with a chirping voice.
I bowed to him once in the palace, shaking his hand.
He was only a man just like me,
A mortal with an expiration date on his breath.
When mine expires, we'll meet again, perhaps
On a more equal term—in death, all men are created equal.

His life-sized statue is taller and imposing,
Standing authoritarian and divine, his hands,
One over the other, humbled not by choice.
He composed music in French, English, Mandarin,
And Khmer about his squalid kingdom, full of mad men
And greedy dictators and oligarchs. The feudal chain
Of French colonial perfume lingering in Ministries.
His back now turned to Independence,
That monument once the tallest, now a miniature figure
Among skyscrapers of modernism.
King and monument, together at last,
Now visited mostly by Koreans and Chinese.

Old Familiars

Roosters crow goodnight and before dawn, perching on a fence, cocking heads, shaking wings to display red, black, and gold aristocratic plumes—arrogant, confident—no war can destroy them.

The entire village is filled with life and natural rhythms and sounds: dogs, wild in hunger, have their time to howl and bark, at any time, night or day, the yelping animals drag suffering, pain, and sorrow on their feet.

To be alive, humans and animals are on constant alert for sustenance. Bony females with sagging breasts roam schoolyards looking for food, only to be stoned as outcasts by mean children bullying even their own kind. These children are schooled to repeat the Khmer alphabet as a mantra, their voices a collective shout of red-flag communist dogma.

The kids' scraggly hair and dirty white-and-blue school uniforms come from poverty, social and economic isolation, rural roads, water buffalo and oxen, plows, rice fields full of water after the monsoon shook heaven with thunder-and-lightning. Toads and bullfrogs join a symphony at night. Crickets and cicadas in the forest, hidden in the banyan trees, tall and thick, the darkness and humidity of life overcrowded and burned by the rush of heat birthing everything to nothing. Boys fly hand-made kites, swim in the muddy pond of their own floating feces, teasing each other, mouth to eyes flirting, tiny bones acrobatic and wiry, gaunt, and stunted by malnutrition.

Every child or cub born to earth is innocent. At play, they are free-spirited and curious, driven by hunger and thirst, in constant joy until bombs fall from the sky. In a war, even birds vanish. Crickets and roosters go silent. In peacetime, the roosters are back where I was born, although I have changed. I know their crows. I am no longer innocent of these familiars amidst roaring tractors and motos churning dust on the road. Home, but never at home with the past.

Sorya the Sun

Bumpy Route 6, Battambang—Poipet,
Mango and banana groves, scent of papaya ousted
From a virgin's breast, her blood old men seek to drink
To remain youthful, this land of pities and insatiable suffering.
Enough of the fallow fields, the lonely houses on stilts,
The exhausting blue skies, past graying noon, heat waves
Into slumbering sleep, combing down like strands of hair.

Thirsty, water and a passion-fruit shake,
Fresh-squeezed orange juice, Fanta of childhood,
Chromosome's last-minute code codified my wanderlust,
Cursed to the life of a vagabond.
In a shared taxi, with women, first female driver
In a male-dominated trade,
Politics and drugs free to discuss among insulated like minds.
Her daughter, an addict, was jailed to get sober and clean.

The reticence of a mule, muteness of a small white elephant,
Marker left from childhood, village and boyhood,
Here, unrecognizable, a miniature carving of a holy creature,
Thought to be Ganesh-born of Shiva's fashion and power.
A shop selling toys and farm tools.
Roadside Depot Tela gas station sits on a buried rice field.
Unleaded is less than two dollars a liter.
Servitude to master is the voice of a motor driver, barking.
New shops, food and gold chains, cell phones the poorest can buy.

Highway, asphalt paved, over a dirt road
Where mother & son took to the market,
Past a roundabout, the elephant in the middle,
Saying hello and bye, the child is said to return—

The elephant waited all this time.
Moto driver stored between his legs my luggage
Full of books in English no one else could read.
He inched past rice fields, left and right, houses big and small,
Shacks and bricked ones, a large public pond where people
Buy their water, stray dogs, and oxen crossing the road.
I looked for a big milk fruit tree, a brown wooden house
Built on cement stilt posts with a tin roof, where the local widow,
Petite, with dark complexion lives. My sister.

In the Poipet district of speeding freedom and progress
Cars and trucks move democracy forward in a country
Once colonized and ruled by absolute power, Father god king
And Mother goddess queen in her squalid and pauper place.
The divide widens between the past and present. Charred leaves
And plastic smoke lift into the ozone. Slash-and-burn agriculture,
Fields and forest on fire, toxins from every house whirl up
Where the widows of war are mending their wounds.
The village's only dirt road floods in the rainy season.

Their older children crossed illegally into Thailand in the night,
Squeezed like sardines for six hours in the back of a truck,
All covered, possibly to suffocate. The unlucky ones die.
The most physically fit survive to slave for bahts they send home
To the widows who watch over their grandchildren.
They become mothers a second or third time,
When they only wish to be free of screaming children
And chanting Pali to their death.
Wrapped in white like old nuns, they prayed
To be reborn into the better life they've earned.
One life after another, the same cycle, full of wishes to be good,
As if to be reborn is to pay for the crimes of a past life
Which they know nothing about.

The widows tell me how they had to run from guns and bombs,
From one firing squad to the next, hiding in trenches, waiting
For the war to quiet down so they could eat and sleep.
A stray bullet bounced and hit one woman, entering
Her left shoulder and throat. She lost her voice and now whispers:

> Husband died of an illness.
>
> Husband died of starvation.
>
> Husband died during the Khmer Rouge genocide.
>
> Husband shot dead by a thief in the night.
>
> Husband died by stepping on a landmine.
>
> Husband died of a curable disease
>
> (no clinic or hospital to treat him on time).
>
> Husband died of high blood pressure.
>
> Husband died of TB.
>
> Husband died of malaria.
>
> Husband died of AIDS.
>
> Husband died of diabetes.
>
> Husband died and left me with nothing.

The Rent

Another thoughtless decision to regret. Desperation battled domination. I signed the short-term rent at two hundred a month. The renter claimed merit for such a reduced rate. First month deposit and a copy of my American passport. Suitcase in a tuk-tuk. Dragged up a flight of narrow stairs to key-enter the house I hadn't inspected. Inside, I wept at the smell of an open sewer. I searched for dead rats under the bed and kitchen sink. I sank low, a phone empty of friends, the heat enormous. Hard road ahead, cleaning a house vacant for years. But a fresh stench of rotting corpses. Ghosts loomed over me, hovering, Ha, ha, I told you so.

Tell me there wasn't a murder here. Domestic violence is common here, but a murder? Though the former torture prison is just a block away. Dead dirt and cobwebs thickened the tiled floor. Out, rusting stains. Free me from the window bars. Where can I escape to? What am I to do with these dungeon-curved stairs, large rooms, an empty hallway, high ceiling, with nothing but rat droppings? Air out the smell by opening windows with the iron bars. Sweep the ceiling of soot, scour the floor, kitchen counter, cabinets, and bathroom tiles until I see sparks.

I dropped to the floor thinking of all I had lost. Running a bar turned out to be a scam. Thousands lost, the fruit of my sweat in an American orchard. Nights on the couch after the last customer at the bar. I was broke. Monkeys from the palace tightrope-walked on electrical wires, ignoring the noisy street, pollution, and garbage, cars and motos honking. All these shops and restaurants barely made enough to pay a worker. Weddings are sad, and funerals are happy. Death to love and life won to end miseries. Their music of equal caliber and volume screamed in my ears. I cursed the dead, cursed the bride and groom to a weeklong diarrhea run.

The humidity thickened with smog. Nights without stars, but dim streetlights, gold to greed. What vengeance to befall my lonely night, as I slept with my thoughts so far ahead of myself, running backward, rewinding the past in search of a future, the hard bed and thin mattress hurting my back, the mosquito net suppressed breath. Nightmare of dislocation, roots pulled up. Oh, how I missed America.

There is no will here to share the bounty of life, no matter how many human-rights marches in London or Phnom Penh. Here, the dominant few have the army and the police on their side to spill more blood, to beat and bleed the populace, the old and the weak, robbing them of land and home, taking rent for a dirty shithole, claiming merits for their next life as thieves and plunderers in the hereafter. I left the owner what peace I had, what loneliness and despair I could leave behind. I left her and her dishonest comrades' prayers for a tortuous death. Farewell, streets of garbage. Take your sewer and choke. I left what illness all the pharmacy money can't cure. This land, this country, sold to the rats and dogs of the future. Take your rent to your kingdom of peril. My cleaning service is free.

How to be Khmer

You need ties and friends, relatives advised.
Ties and affluence to influence and uphold the status quo,
Wearing foreign designer's suit, passenger seat, in a Lexus.
Money can buy a private driver.

Design your own villa copied from foreign soap-opera magazines
On whose covers foreign aristocrats speak English.
Seek Western alliances to school your children,

Build efficient roads to weather the monsoon rain.
If you want to get ahead give yourself to the current,
Bend and flow to corruption and immorality.
Make allies with oppressors and display your aggression
To earn respect with bought-weapons from ambassadors.

Slowly, you can rise to the top.
Keep your ears open, mouth agape, like a beggar.
In high fashion, work your kingdom of charms for NGO money.
Help! We are Khmer Rouge genocide victims, wretched and poor.
Hear the powerful truth of the illiterates
And foreign money—the truly educated silenced.
Gold treasure and heritage incites from their lips lies and untruths.
What the illiterates say can't be argued. What they can't write
Can't be rewritten; set in stone, a path, intolerant of divergence.
Democracy lip-service glossed over by the so-called "civilized" ones.
Their human rights behind closed doors of embassies.
Unwilling to defy tyrants they helped put in place.

Do not speak against the regime.
Do not let anyone know that you're reading criticisms about it.
Keep it to yourself. Lie in clandestine darkness with your thoughts

And freedom of speech, emboldened by the stars and moon
In your own private dream-room.
Go sing your discontent in bars and nightclubs, karaoke,
With young virgins holding your microphone.
Your dance partners who don't have political views,
Neutral to any metaphors you dare express.
Drink National Angkor Beer owned by a private enterprise.
The Khmers who built the temple are long dead.
Don't go where you can't enter. High-walled fences,
Spikes and glass shards mean Stay Out.

Don't give yourself headaches thinking about
What you can't see or control.
Help yourself first, so that you can help someone else.
If "it" doesn't affect you, whatever "it" is,
Don't let someone else's madness make you unhappy.
Get married so you can have children to care for you
When you're old and decrepit. Avoid politics at all costs.
Be kind to others, so others will be kind to you.
What comes around goes around.
If you want to get somewhere, you need affiliates and
Approval from your proper class, an education
Into the proper distinction and social status.
Beware of users, and don't speak if you have nothing to say.

A Badge of Praise, a Title to State

An Identity or an identifier, Khmer introduced and reintroduced, a writer, an artist, poems, poets, visual or photographic; filmmaker, there are award festivals in the world. Dawning a new dawn, artistic Cambodia on the prize. We have arrived. It's about time.

Hi, I am a writer.
You write what?
I scratch my head.
Melodrama, I said.

There's drama in the amount of precipitation and rainfall. Climate change is rarely heard here. I am interested in birds of paradise as architects of the forest. The intersection between pornography and empty arrogance at the eve of fame and notoriety. I like titles and carrying my badge of praise. As I said, I am a writer.

I write Karaoke (empty Orchestra in Japanese). K-Pop Koreans in short skirts, light dims, kisses sniffing scents, pheromones (roses, Jasmine and frangipani in the dark). That's how we prefer IT.

Light off. Countryside, palm juice, peasant and low class, not knowing how to touch and feel, prohok and krasang stenches sour, light on.

Me love you long time, wanting land and riches, invasion folded into factors of bribes and gifted brides, espionage, taking over Khmer men spreading ancient map drawn by the French, empirical as reclamation of past kingdoms now lost to foreign women who knew the trade of physical desire, using their own Kamasutra to Indochinese and more.

Talk about globalized sex trade long ago. It's as old as evolution from ape to man. Thumbs to tools as sex to war and peace, invasion and conquests, colonialism and French baguettes, their sex superior in the open, on rice field ground, dogs and man, the buffaloes and oxen grazing on pleasure, reproductive organs.

Here, it's best to wear a surgical mask against dust and fumes. Ebola is a possibility, a potential threat. Transcontinental Coronaviruses viral in the air, shrapnel of past and ongoing wars, in other countries and lands, the lack of jobs has fueled violence in the name of god.

I am a writer, I said.

I don't know what you write, but we can't be writing about the same thing. We can't understand each other's facts and figures. We don't have each other's dreams or vision. I can't even see colors. I write green on everything. You see shades of gray, black, and blue, and all these conformities and pretexts to follow, cultural laws and order, architectural wordings and designs, clouds and birds, winged leaves or parasites, my imagination unlike yours doesn't rhyme to jail and morality. I write to educate myself, so I am not adhering to educating others. I am not a teacher. I'm a writer.

If you ask me, I'm actually nobody. I do everything and nothing at the same time. I lie around, smoke American cigarettes, Marlboro if you like, masturbate at my leisure. I don't label myself. My eyes are fierce and sharp, but they don't have the color of the sky. My smiles are sometimes true, but often sad, but I'm free. I am not bounced to anyone's title or praise, shackled by insecurity and boundaries. I have known bombs and heartlessness. I think you're just a good piss and not a very good deep throat.

From a Khmer Poet to Another

Don't forget rhymes and proper stanzas,
The placement of grammatically correct words and phrases.
Be well-versed and an expert in this first before you start to write.

Khmer is ancient, full of beautiful flowers and trees that rulers cut down,
Ways to rhyme and play with words, ways to tell and describe,
The language Angkorian with boundless feats,
Romance and longing it can express,
Where flowers in high degree full of scent and virgin breasts like Apsaras
Bounced to the wall, moon, and stars, rapture a kingdom full of majesties.

You can write, but you must write the way I tell you. It is the correct way.
I have been a poet for a long time. I know everything about poetry.
No one writes like me. I am the only voice
In the history of Khmer literature.
Have you read anyone like me?

No. I can't read and write Khmer. Should I be happy or sad?
The Khmer I can read and write isn't your kind of poem.
In fact, you don't consider it poetry. It doesn't rhyme
Or follow eight-or-four-line restrictions.
I am not a literary expert, not in English or Khmer.
I don't belong to your social class. I am not an educated person,
But I'm a learner.
I don't have a Ph.D. in history or literature.
I just have words my mother taught me.
Hiss like a snake, she told me. Fly and chirp like a bird, she said.
Freedom in the sky, she pointed. Love in my arms.
Speak as if you're whispering to the wind,
As if the ocean had swallowed you inside.
Dream where the dragonflies dance, where fireflies laugh and cry.

Hear your mother's rice fields, in sorrow and in joy,
Swing and sway, dusk to dawn. Drink the milk of her forgiveness,
Lick from her dewdrops the life and wisdom on the morning grass.
Swim in my river, she said. Laugh on your back, float.
From me, a life no one can own or barter,
Proud as the beauty of this inheritable earth,
Where my tongue sharp and blissful, free and bold, boundless,
Can hiss from the heart of a snake.

By Title

Lord-isms walk by title like a crown to a king, his shoulders sharp with badges, the epaulettes of many stars over other generals, Buddhist by birth, his nation's faith, monks in saffron with arrow tongues and tiger fangs. Tribes and clans divide the race, dogs from dogs, by manner of breeds, cats from cats, bird by bird, how to exist, how to judge and name a friend or foe, what caste or social lot to follow and confirm, what demagogue to hurrah and praise, what dawn of history to associate with and what money and power to acquire.

From his throat, a villain's voice slurping beef noodles too hot to swallow. He blows on the succulent meat before addressing the crowd, he takes a sip of Hennessy at a French bar only expats can afford. He even buys his enemies an unwelcome drink to display the power of his fame. The artist with slit eyes and pale light skin was subjugated by the Khmer Rouge. The toiling that bent his father's arrogance now belongs to him. He does not bow to anyone or accept any novice as his student. He's international, he's big, and the price of his work is home, land, and workers. A plantation managed by drivers and hired maids, and lay artisans who craft his designs into sculptures that sell in far-away museums. His American degrees, MFA and English, sly interpretation of abstraction, ways to see light and shadows, the whereabouts of cave paintings, medieval, and European renaissance. He learned from the books, he went to museums, he visited his artist célèbre in France, Van Gogh in his grave, the American West of avant-gardes to the realism of Mexican artists, the murals of America's south, the peasant the Khmer Revolutionists wanted to emulate and who, like Mao, would eradicate the artists who paint suffering.

The only painter to survive the torture prison was the one who could paint a portrait of Pol Pot. Past evil returns in full swing, the arrogance of fame and fortune, the look-downs of the rich upon the poor, the judgment and tribalism, all the Lord-isms, badges, and epaulettes of honor and social status, Lexus and land cruisers, window down, spitting barbarism.

The American education system isn't required to teach humility. Students have to learn it themselves, and often not. They mirror the very evil that evil seeks to eradicate, one mass grave at a time, one killing field to the next, one Rwanda and Kosovo to the other. The louder the bark, the clearer the hawking, the greater the hubris to kill—and the poor, bitter and uneducated, can only steer the arrows, trigger the guns, wave the red flag, beyond reason, the karmic wheels taking their churns, one educated to another, eating cow dung, collecting feces. This forced onto them by the same people with equal footing, who learned from foreign shores the idea to colonize and suppress each other and their own people. With the rise of the peasant class they stirred to pick up the machetes, the axes, and the guns.

The hours of vengeance start with the spitting and arrogance of the Lord-isms. They know nothing about human hearts, the ups and downs of life. The fervent pride of an illiterate, once he's powered and named, produces the blood the artist can use as his paint. The educated, like children, are too quick to profess what they know, too quick to call out names, too dismissive of those who haven't had the opportunity to open a book.

One day... said a moto driver... one day... history will repeat itself.

The Life of Ochnya Yang Ly Hai

Excellency, Ochnya Yang Ly Hai is fictional, but he walks among us since Zhou Daguan came to Angkor Wat. Mingling, mixing, and populating rites and rituals, fates and philosophies, cross-calculating time and money. We know him today as trade and free enterprise, marketing of silks along ancient roads, elephants made to carry kings and queens, princes to and from wars. Defending their kingdom from foreign invasions and conquests. Dancing dragons, fireworks and dynamite. Fat Buddha and martial art. Feng Shui to rightly place an altar, a body of water, an object to bring luck and fortune, a statue looking into the mirror. Habitats of human reflection and deflection of evil, good ridding of the bad, money and power banked to greater happiness.

Natural harmony encircling a family of wealth and knowledge, hard working from rags to riches. His Excellency lived a very good life. He worked hard to guarantee all his forebears a great fortune. He's ready to die. A fifty thousand-dollar badly carved lion has been installed to protect his tomb. On a mound, remote from the city, in the rural rice fields, a mausoleum has been prepared, made of heavy teak, the wooden coffin in which his dead body shall be buried sitting up. A mummy awaits his next life of greater power and wealth than the last. His name, his date of birth and the day he died in large Mandarin script. Mourning him with plastic flowers, and his favorite beer, Chinese dumplings and noodles, Nom Poow (steamed dough stuffed with pork), the relatives toast and praise him for his good deeds. They recall hereditary and ancestral achievements, an empire he built, a name people fear and respect.

Heaven opens. Hell for the garment workers protesting for more money. Riot police shoot tear gas. Bulleted democracy replaced with Maoist, Khmer Rouge aggression. It's not China, but he came to rule another country just like it. The price of his tomb could feed a village for five years—and the villagers would take no money to build his tomb. They carried his heavy coffin to be placed inside the hollowed den. What he spent on the tomb, a million huts for the poor. Go for the golden tomb, the expensive teak, and the ill-carved lion to roar him past his greed, into the heavenly clouds, in his private Lexus, the metal bird blowing smoke up his ass.

The Killing of an Ochnya (Excellency)

That's where an Ochnya was shot and killed, said my moto driver.
He pointed past a crowd of cars and motos. Where? I tried to
picture where he was pointing. I couldn't see as he kept pointing
ahead. The driver stopped at a traffic light, on red. Here, he said.
This very spot! He pointed down. I started to see blood on the
asphalt. My heart raced like the shooter's. I felt the bullets like the
victim did.

But because Ochnya was synonymous with the rich and an
oppressor in my mind, I felt more the rage and anguish of the
shooter. Maybe that Ochnya deserved it, I thought.

I witnessed it, said the driver. Where were you when you heard
the shot? I asked. For a moment, I thought I had heard JFK's
assassin. Robert Kennedy, Martin Luther King, and Gandhi. Here,
where I stopped on red. I looked up at the red light, waiting for
green. All I could see was blood.

Where was the Ochnya? I asked. He was in his car stopped on
red. A young man walked up to him, and "Bang," he shattered the
windshield at point blank. The murderer went for the Ochnya's
head and then his heart and his groin.

How do you know all this? I asked. I was here, he pointed down.
It's green, I said. He proceeded.
Would you kill anyone? I asked straight ahead.
You never know, he said. It all depends on the circumstances.

He would kill, I thought.
I can tell by the look on his face and in his eyes.
He has the face of a Khmer Rouge soldier

Or a Vietcong I had pictured as a child, when fear of them
Was ingrained in my head.

You can say you won't kill anyone, he said.
But you're fooling yourself.
What if someone tries to kill your family?
Someone who pushes you to a point where you have no choice?
I pondered his question for a moment.

I still can't kill, I told him.
He laughed.
I know a man who wouldn't kill a fly,
But he killed another man.
I changed my mind about killing.
Someone had tried to kill me before.
I was beaten and bound, hands to my back.

Once you've killed,
He continued, you'll be a killer for life. There's no turning back.
I thought he was clever and wise.
Khmers say blood screams for blood, skin calls for skin.
What do you mean? I asked.

Once you've killed, you will never be able to sleep.
The dead are dead gone, but you, the killer, suffer from conscience.
Maybe someday, someone else will kill him
Like he killed the Ochnya, he explained.

He took a sharp left turn in traffic, slowly among honking cars.
A driver spoke on his phone, inching ahead, blocking traffic.

Can you say for sure that you can't kill? he asked.

I didn't answer.
I imagined jabbing someone with a knife, how the knife
Would sound when it hits the bones, bones breaking,
The sound of blood spurting out, and how that life
Would flee, in the fresh air, taking this pollution with it
And from the body life running free.
I went off the wall. God, I prayed,
Don't ever let me kill. I want a normal life and death.

MOTHER, I'M COMING HOME

Mother, I'm Coming Home

Sixteen years is too long.
Mother, I'm coming home
To collect your bones.

The war that killed your husband is through.
The killing fields are done.
I still wake to the sounds of guns.

Sixteen years is too long.
I am home, mother, to collect your bones.

Your voice telling me to run:
Run, run, run 'til you're free,
Run as far as you can.
When the war's over,
We shall meet again.

I look for you in the things I had known—
Bamboo bush and the mango trees you had grown.
There's nothing but despair in your bones.

Run from the firing squads of heartless men.
Go where you'll be safe.
You'll grow up to have better days.
Return when you can.
We will soon meet again.

I am home, mother, to collect your bones.

The Happiest Day

Look to the rivers for calm, to the sky for inspiration.
Birds for free flight. Hear the cicadas' love and humanity.
Weep in memory of joy, the sound of a bamboo flute, a tro or chepey,
The old music and dance of lives taken and a culture maimed.
Doves drop olive branches of the Paris Peace Accords,
Everywhere, white flags wave, people lay down weapons and dance.
Freedom drums in a marching band.
The King sings karaoke in his palace.
Rain patters the city's tin, straw, and thatches absent war's fire.

Count the people's votes.
The ruling party is crooked,
But the elected king's brother must bend,
His power is shared. Peace no matter the cause.
Millions have been lost,
& look how long it will take to heal the broken,
How little resources at hand rebuild the shattered.
Can't waste time. Choose life, not death.
Cocks crow, clearing their throats of tear-choked breaths.
Eyes meeting the sun, they perch on high posts,
Pronouncing the arrival of peace governed by an elected official.

Take the Mekong, still on course after many wars,
After the bombs and grenades, feces and garbage dumped in her.
She flows in natural pushes and pulls of time and weather,
The fanfare of inhumanity weeping at her shore,
These people quenching their thirst with her generosity,
Bathed in her flow to scour away their pain.

Young and old lovers return hand-in-hand as buildings, hotels,
And residences are built, rebuilt, renovated in light of progress.

Cafés and shops full of people, coming and going, sipping wine,
A future without helicopters, B-52s, Chinese-and-Russian-mines.
Without beggars missing a hand or a leg, an eye, without birth defects,
Maggot-infested wounds of the heart that beats and feeds the flies.

The happiest day of buried sorrow
Came with new violence and political oppression,
The rise of powerful individuals above the law,
Fall of human morality and agreement. Distrust of conquest.
Peace came with brothels, a flesh market for peacekeepers
And local men who pluck young virgin breasts from poor villages,
A dollarization of innocence in a country molested.
Defenders of independence now beg.

The divine king revealed to be an ordinary old boring man.
His magic doesn't work. He can't heal his nation.
He can't mend broken ancient temples.
Private companies control tourist money.
Freedom and security remain tender,
As Khmer Rouge incursions disturb the peace daily in the re-start,
People learn how to live without weapons of mass destruction.
Hope chants, "Let doves fly forever over Kampuchea.
Let the pigeons shit on the palace rooftops.
Feed them boiled peanuts and French baguettes."

Western domination returned. Chinese economic hegemony.
Aid and debt returned. Japanese brought cars and bridges.
Khmer are free, but chained to foreign peacekeepers and money.
Rebuilding means cutting down the forest, selling land for development,
Mining more gemstones and gold, blasting mountains for roads.
The lakes filled with sewage—double the feces.
It's rich versus poor, trading innocent flesh for men's pleasure.

Happy to be home, nostalgic, and in tears, on a moto,
Driving on a mud-sticking road in a red-light district, Tuol Kork,
Past the French Embassy, the glory of Phnom Penh slow and sad,
Beating to shaky progress, quick money-making, nepotism and corruption,
Tenuous democracy disguised in a new form of tyranny,
One-party one-man rules, one family against the rest,
The poor left to the stench of their own shit and air pollution.
Phnom Penh lights at night. On occasion, fireworks and boat races,
Music, weddings, deaths, the old dying for the young to breathe
Into them the courage and independence to make their own time.
Peace must live and grow with them or nothing will flower.
No one will care about the stars.

The New Cambodia

A man and his machine move a load of bouncing pigs
Squeezed tightly in a bamboo basket on the back of his moto.
Chicken passengers strung beak down, legs tied to wooden bars.
Another man holding a sheet of glass while a friend drives.
A man on a heap of mangoes sleeping as the truck honks in traffic.
Children perched on daddy's lap while he drives, the mother behind.
Cars take road space, in a hurry, pounding their horns.

It's hard to like anyone who drives a Lexus or a Hummer.
Hard to avoid massive Range Rovers, SUVs blowing smoke.
One man or a woman to a car, slowly inching in traffic.
This is progress. We know wealth and power.
Machines symbolize man's greatest achievements.
His money can buy whatever he wants.
Everything we don't produce, there's a desire waiting for it.
Once bicycles and pedestrians, cyclos or rickshaws, now big cars,
Motos and tuk-tuks taking people somewhere, home, from work,
To market, the roar of harmony or chaos, new sound of Phnom Penh,
Death-sirens, three dead a day, blood on asphalt, tar melting.

We move on, continue, forward, leaping into the future,
Never turning, will never turn back, just go, flow with the current,
Go with the traffic, don't stop, don't hesitate,
Make something out of your life,
Do something for a change, don't be stagnant. Don't dwell on your pain.
Suffering comes, as Buddha says, with a body.
Just think about survival, think about life,
What you can do to live a good life. Stay in motion,
Look ahead, don't fret with the past, stay focused on the future,
The present is now. How to be rich? How to be free?
Is just another form of oppression.

The point is not to think, but to live—
In spite of everything, we are not going to be stuck in traffic.

Bamboo Bush/Kapok Tree

Returning,
Sixteen years of smells and sounds.
A Cambodia/Campuchea of a different time.
No, neither guns nor exploding bombs.
They tell me
Phnom Penh is full of people.
I've forgotten. I've read of emptiness.
Weddings and deaths.
They tell me
I could never understand the destruction wrought
They tell me.
I left on foot,
Hunted in Thailand on the way to America.
We were fleeing toward safety and fame, away from war and genocide.
Nothing is familiar
About my home—the river drove on
The Kapok tree my mother had planted.
My sister had told me to look for a bush of bamboo,
But they are everywhere, and how could she remember
If I couldn't—I asked an old man Grandfather if he
Knew my sister Sareen, and shaking he didn't know my
Father Uy Lam. Everyone knows him, and I am
His youngest son but fingers point north farther on
Toward a woman squatting under a Kapok Tree not asking
Questions about mangoes or bamboo.
The missing fence and house not embraceable, but my mother's
Voice echoes back from the market
Past a broken bridge where a machine gun was searching
For an idyllic view.
No house. No pond. No bamboo.
No lemon grass.

Daem Kor, the Kapok Tree

Rooted deepest in the bank of Stung Sangker, your shade taking the sun, from where I look I am the tiniest of creatures, admiring you, tree of time, smooth bark of green, shape of light caressing you among bamboos and low canopy trees, you are my witness.

Here, I arrived ignorant of local ways, their love and their hatred, their greed & self-destruction that you have seen during my absence, a son who had gone far and not forgotten your goodness. I return to take refuge in your grandeur and power, to hear and to see the sky.

My arms wide open, kneeling before you, tell me who is out here I can love and trust. Show me to the river, where it begins & ends, what songs, what stories it can share, all ears, all eyes, envisioning a time of peace. May this country return to kindness & community.

I'd like to build a tiny home to put my heart at rest when I am lonely & sad. I can find safety in your protection, my tears for your strength. Give me this chance once, I won't ask of you anymore.

Take me back home

to die a true son,

never again in horror or nightmare should I ever have to run.

City of Moving Flesh

City of moving flesh,
Eden of rats,
madness of engines,
press & press for time,
marching onward,
unpaved road of walkers,
lights, dots in black,
call my name to retreat & hide among you,
the smallest your grandeur swallows,
press the pressing, out of time,
the aged gone, goodbye, leaving
the night to the young,
in cars, on motos & in tuk-tuks,
who breathe the smothering breaths,
dislodge & discharge resistance, onward in the current,
these bodies are on the prowl, on the hunt,
ritz and glamour,
development & progress collide head-on
with the conscience of souls in the dead, in the living room.
The city of flesh trade, making babies with poverty
to kill each other for wealth,
so many mouths to feed,
so many thirsty throats to satisfy,
alive, but tired & dead inside,
where to go,
but sit & wait for another day of sunlight on my face
in gratitude & in praise of the day
I can join a marching band, drum for drum.
I hum the body electric of every fate.

Men are Gold, Women are Cloth: Sary's Story

"When I was five, I lived with a woman I called Auntie. She shoved hot rice porridge in my face.

"Eat it! She shouted and spat. She called me stupid with her index finger to my forehead for being on top of my class. She even accused me of tempting her son for sex.

"My family saved her family from the murdering Khmer Rouge. To pay us back, she invited me to live with her. She said I could go to school after I cleaned her house and cooked her meals. I swept and mopped the floor, fetched water from a faraway river to fill her urns and washed the dishes after all her family ate. I slept standing up in her kitchen. I woke up at 4 a.m. to start my chores. She was still unhappy.

"My teacher said I must sell snacks for her while other children took breaks and played. During recess, I stayed behind to erase and clean the blackboard.

"My mother had nothing when my father left us for another woman. She died of a broken heart, alone at Calmette Hospital. The doctor didn't treat her because she had no one to guarantee payment. I was too busy surviving, hustling in the dungeon of bars and restaurants to run for her last words, what breaths of hope she could spare.

"As a condition for keeping my job, the bosses said I had to sleep with customers. Barang of all shapes and sizes could touch our breasts. They had dollars to order our bodies outside the menu. But I did not comply. I knew a ten-year-old girl whose mother sold her to foreign men for three hundred dollars each turn. She shriveled in pain and she shook after the rapes. I hugged and cried with her.

"Growing up, I had no one. I had to rely on myself for hope and strength. I had to hustle to live. I went to Malaysia to work, where I was treated like a dog. I slept standing up and started work at 4 a.m.

for no pay. The Chinese Malaysian family beat me, jailed me in their kitchen cell, and had me arrested when I ran away to escape their torture and cruelty. Eventually, I escaped the Chinese and managed to get home.

"At home, the agent who sold my labor tried to put me in jail. He said I had no right to escape. It was my responsibility to remain a slave. Many girls weren't as lucky as me. They were tortured and raped. Some killed themselves. Others came home without a mind. Just bodies as wandering ghosts.

"Where I call home, ignorance rules. The blind see. The illiterate are noble. Men are gold and women are just pieces of cloth. The rich own the poor. Men buy virgins, bleeding ten-years-olds. Poverty and war stole our childhood. I had to become a bitch, Khmer howling. I eyed the moon, plucked the tail of some stars, wishing and wishing, one day, I would avenge all my scars. Avenging was what I did, with my smarts and education, I survived. No matter how great the cruelty, however hard the struggle, I wanted to stay alive—alive with a mind and a heart beating, learning how to read love from hate and peace from war.

"My consciousness is that of an individual and survivor. I survived rape and beating. Exploitation. Jail. Falsely accused of tempting males when I had no idea what sex was, but I was a whore, a piece of cloth and simply a vagina. The other bitches with money and rich husbands pulled my hair, threw me against the wall, kicked and slapped me, screaming I had wooed their sons. Our compassion for each other was gone. Some foreigners saw this and took the opportunity to prey. Local men were their sycophants and middlemen. Everyone was dealing and trading the female flesh.

"Once a virgin was bled, she was no longer worthy of another rape. She became just a number hiding behind a white-powdered mask in squalid brothels where cheap, local boys went for sex as a rite of passage. I escaped this fate. A Khmer-American ran a bar where I worked. Unlike other people I met, he didn't try to sell my virginity to foreigners. I did what I could to stay away from the brothel. I lived with a friend near an open sewer. Our toilet was a small hole we dug. We had to buy water to bathe and drink.

"I've learned that being smart is not normal for a Khmer girl like me. I am only worth what my vagina is worth in the meat market. However intelligent I may be, this miserable country won't raise or encourage me to own my vision. My breasts are heaving with bitterness and vengeance. I take revenge by self-educating, working hard to become the woman I want to be. Khmer traditions have favored the male dogs. I was born only to spin around the kitchen like a domestic worker. I am to be torn and shredded, to be dressed and undressed, in the dark, fighting as the rape began.

"Expect humans to rape and pillage. Vultures are everywhere. The birds want to peck at your flesh. Your humanity is sewage. The carnage of the past stinks up the present. Ill intents can be disguised in kindness. They copy your intelligence and boast to others that it is theirs. Schools don't teach you how to think, how to be fair and just. Teachers teach you how to be part of the corruption, lie and cheat. The leaders are for themselves. The uneducated run universities and public schools. The teachers teach children to follow and serve them. Society teaches you to measure yourself by class, rich from poor, men from women, how to devalue your worth, and how not to dream and reach for the stars. No one had taught me to feel proud. I taught myself through the mirror of hatred and violence.

"I am no proper Khmer woman. I'm rolling up my sleeves and my pants, wearing short skirts and high heels, lipstick and rouge like a prostitute. These men with a penis the size of my pinky finger— just give them the beer, the Lexus and Hennessy. Give them the Rolex watch. They fart and shit like everyone else. Don't think for a second just because I am a woman you can buy and sell me. I am not for sale although some white women think I'm after their white men. They seem surprised that I can think and that I have a job. A white man I was with thought he could beat me like the local men do. He took away my rights to rear my child. I had to run from the bruises of his domination. My daughter is gone now. There's not a day I don't think about her. The daughter I cannot raise to become as strong as me. I hope she'll return to hear my explanation, and that she will forgive me for the absence she felt, forgive me for the missing lullabies."

Why Did I Come Back?

Why did you come back?
For the same reasons you stayed.
The umbilical cord tied
To land and country.
My attempt to reconnect
With what I had known,
To fill the void.
Maybe it was time.
I fled when I was ten.
I never met my father.
I lack shared memories.
I needed a home and people
To whom I belong
A mother tongue to speak and
A culture to know.
Maybe I want to understand why I left.
The genocide?
What cruelty had I witnessed?
Skulls and skeletons filling the map.
The living deafened and scared.
Memories of hunger and thirst.
Where I was born, people still cry.
In the killing fields where tourists visit,
Tears are shed.
There's no marking to stake my claim.
Any traces of Khmer are buried deep inside me.
I survived.
I'm here.
Why did I come back to this country of sorrow?

The Saddest of the Sad

I must be the saddest.
My eyes fixed on certain disturbances, crying for no reason.
I am sad because all the people I see are sad.
The sun is bright but sad.
Sadness in my hair, inside my bones,
On my pillow and inside the sheet I wrap over my skin.

Exposed, these vulnerable limbs fear everything,
Even laughter. They fear revulsion & rejection.
I think of unannounced visits of strangers.
I address them as older brothers or sisters.
I fear men who stake claim to me as their nephew.
I am afraid to be seen wearing dollar pants & shirt,
When all I ever wanted was a home & country
And a people to love and call friends.

No one visits if I have nothing but myself.
No one wants to be with a heart-breaker,
No one wants to be betrayed.
It's difficult to be here, land & country of broken hearts,
Without toys to craft a viable future out of poverty.
Here, the saddest of sad walks around in search of a true friend,
But everyone is too involved in buying & selling.
When they can't sell, they are sad.

The saddest takes comfort in routine,
The dreaming & the waking hours of anticipation,
Wanting & needing to be held, the daily task of feeding.
Something in it isn't right or isn't there.
My body roofed & protected, but I'm sad,
Like a shadow that doesn't need light to cast it.

Frequent Flyer Guest, Phnom Penh 2016

Checking out. Checking in
I am now the motherland's frequent-flyer guest.
Birth country I had fled.
An American passport pockets dollars home.
I was a refugee running.
Running from where my mother had bled,
Giving birth to me kicking and screaming.
Babies were victims here.
The smell of blood fresh,
Like yesterday,
Like bullets,
Like burning flesh.
Frights are goosebumps in the humid blue sky.

No. Not here.

Here, I remember villages of family members
Turned enemies through indoctrination.
Broken hearts of severed love.
Familial ties in reverse: children now the rulers
And killers (forced to break the bond).
Here, a temple's holy ground is a killing field.
Temple caves where dead babies were dropped.
Women, after a rape, had been shoved down to hell.
Monks forced to disrobe to gather cow dung
To fertilize Pol Pot's rice fields.
Old people declared senile and useless, killed.
Blood redder than red filling the Mekong River.
Tears and rain turned the color of metallic clay.

Here, nothing is ever over.
Nightmares upon nightmares recurring and recurring,
Old wounds surfacing are vengeful and bitter.
Someone will rise again,
Someone will take hold to declare independence
From something or someone.
Someone will wriggle free of repression and oppression
And more blood-spilling.
Every regime replaces patrons and guests,
Who clothe old habits of war and violence
Under the guise of democracy.
Greetings and formalities are demagogues
Wearing dollar signs.

I checked out. I am checking in.
But I can't do it with the past.
Wounds linger.
I'm frightened of falling bombs replacing the joyful monsoon.

The Circle of Life

Rarely does a rich one marry a poor one.
In each other's likeness the knots are tied,
Impoverished to the impoverished,
In sickness or in health, groom over bride.
A process of mourning begins early,
Megaphone blast to all the villagers, this music
Of false love bearing reproductive sorrow.

Crickets and frogs sense what is near while the distant wedding
Is unclear and loud. Whether the lyrics are blessing or curses—
The shouting and screaming filled the air like thick rain.

The bride in fear of the groom, the man of doom and gloom,
Will assume his role as her dominator, her ruler man of the house,
Once first love is gone, the fretting and the shouts begin,
His demands and commands.
It's culture and tradition, the natural order of thing,
The proper rite of passage, familial pressure pushing, pulling,
Blind leading blind, illiterates trying to decipher codes.
Why does any girl, any woman, slave away her life?
Settled to a small existence, they blindly begin a family.

For some it may be love, for others it may be love turning hate.
Bruises and broken bones. Why then do they hurry to marry?
It must be animal lust instinct, a primordial need to procreate,
Just the way it is, marry to marry, a family to inherit pots and pans,
Maybe a thatched-roof house, a genetic disease,
A dirt road to nowhere,
A ladder to faith in the sky,
A higher being to set you free.

Roses are red and love is blue—what madness you create,
That madness looks back at you.

My Father on His Face

My uncle has my father's face. Short, his jawbone's sharp like a tiger's. I hug and pick him up like I would my father, whom I have no memory of as a child. The skin slides from his bones when I touch it, like silky paper. His eyes clouded with cataracts the color of rice porridge. He's age ninety with a broken hip from painting his house. My aunt blames him for not retiring. He worked all his life in and out of markets, carrying loads of beans for his wife to sell. His children are far away. But each time I see him, he's happy. I buy him fruit and I give him cash—this time for his hip treatment: the traditional Khmer medicine, wrapped in gauze bandages around his left thigh up to his waist.

He wishes he could fly somewhere with his wife. He hasn't even been to Angkor Wat. After the Khmer Rouge, Phnom Penh had been his world. He asked about a plane and America. He remains the only resemblance: my father's eyes and Chinese nose. I tenderly touch his arms and feet. His own children are distant. He's a burden to them, he's draining their inheritance and money they don't have on his hip treatment. I wish I had known him like I could have known my father—

I would wrap my short arms around him a thousand times. Feel every part of his face and know every strand of his hair. Kiss his eyes and listen to his heart.

If only my father was here, I would know earth beneath sky, the joy of sorrow in his shawl, the way I've known love from another man. My umbilical cord was a genetic warranty of human goodness.

Failed Beans

My nephew's crop of beans and cucumbers failed. The rats ate his entire labor's worth. He sits on a stump, eyeing the sky, with a cheap cigarette between his fingers, Scheming another plan—his back to his loved ones. He's skin and bones, short but muscular like his father. When his father was shot dead, he was two, like me when my father was killed.

I gave him money for this piece of land, which he barely fills in with a few mango trees. His tin house is like an oven during the hot season. The pond he pumps water from for his crop is drying up. He uses a solar panel for electricity. He, his five-year-old daughter, and wife live in this tiny tin house he built with the money I provided. He traps rats and skins them to sell as tidbits men eat with beer and homemade medicinal alcohol. The men rant about whiskey and the current regime.

They say the opposition party would have better helped the rural poor. Most young people in border villages go to Thailand to work. Thai jobs keep them from starving. Grandparents care for small children.

Every night, my nephew sits. When he needs something, he won't tell me because he's afraid that I would be upset or be pressured to help him. He plans things in his head, each day, like counting grains of rice in a pot he is about to cook. He looks to the sky, he looks away, but straight into my eyes, and he looks downward and sighs, as if his heart and mind had shrunk of muses, solutions, or clarifications. If I really want to help him, I should help develop an idea that he likes and work on with him until he can keep himself and his family alive.

His mother is sometimes the source of help. She sits alone in her thoughts, staring into space.

She has all these events replaying in her mind. She lives a life of many reincarnations, many ties to land and memory, accounting for who did what to whom. Good versus evil is evident in her daily life, her Buddhist chant. At night, she places a burning incense stick every direction in the house, like my mother used to do, and in her altar, with a Chinese inscription she can't read, and she recites a mantra in Khmer that I don't understand. I would go to sleep in the cloud of her smoldering incense. In the afternoon, she watches a Chinese soap opera. In the evening, she chooses a Filipino sitcom. Now, there are Khmer programs that are actually really good. I started to watch them with her, and she would say, remember this and that, when we were kids?

I nodded.

BODY &

SOUL

The Body Electric

After Walt Whitman

Electrified, I am electric,
body and soul,
I enter the hands of time he has moved & touched,
where I have felt
silk & bark of trees
against my bare back.

I am not alone
but visible,
where dreams roam for a body to inhabit,
streets and fanfares,
confetti, songs and dances
People—

a gathering of birds,
watchers follow—ornithological
& anthropological,
man and behaviorist & timekeeper,
high in allusions, but
delusional,

offering to be received,
to be offered,
a surrendering, a sacrifice,
a life free
bathed in light
drifts far into fantasy.

Heart at rest, river of pulses
flows west to east,

wingspan & mileage,
this body travels
in & out of dreams
& realities.

Life of a pauper & a king,
Parisian at dawn,
a rooftop cave, eyes into fog—
sleeting, but never snow,
electrified on the go,
the Parisian body bathed in gold.

Leaves of Rice

What's nesting in your old white beard?
Leaves of rice, a trillion grains of lice undressing the husks,
Peeling away the inflection of desire, lies exposing truth?
Beautiful celebrator of torsos and thighs, old man in the sea,
Where feminine forms absorb from the masculine, a gentility
Perfected by Michelangelo, reaching God on the Sistine ceiling.

You could have written about soldiers who disarmed each other.
From enemies to comrades in satin sheets,
Wild in dreams encircling their brows,
Hope bending to stars, what howls of pleasure reaching Mars!
Gentle claws gripped the earth to fill rivers with blood.
The tiniest particles noticed, from the root of each strand of hair
To the pubis of moss, the contraction of lips, thirsty, moist—
Settle differences for a harmony of the flesh, the jerking fair use of
Beauty that the masculine bears, the weighty secrets in your lairs.

Men you had coveted with your eyes. Boys the bluest sky
Could have plucked from a goddess's protection.
I read the slightest movement of your heart,
What arrow and ready sling it had aimed, a chest of pulses and impulses,
Those witnesses of the spell-bound bodies you cast from paradise.

White poet, you sang the body electric, you sang of faraway places
Where soldiers roamed. You talked of wounds splaying
Lions and tigers,
The peeling of oppression,
The liberation of the flesh, birth and death of flowers,
What leaves of grass whispering, one masculine ear to another.
A succession of truths you hid for the plums and the apples of Eden.

Adam came first, between you and him,
The artist in the sky who chiseled you into being,
How he had touched you, bathed you from stone
Into warm supple flesh,
His holy nails parting your hair,
Goldilocks, the curls he carved
Before he blew you the breath
To forget that he loved you first.
Don't forget it. The body of your brother belongs to him only,
Which is why you took your brother's hand, song by song.
Sing it, old man, sing the body electric,
Rice and wheat growing in your white beard.

A Crossroads

What tongue must speak today?
What road must a traveler's heart choose?
Paint me a picture of you stuck in a dream.
Call Jung to explain your indecision and despair.
There, where longing is shortened and cut off,
You mistook me for someone else.
But what doubt had driven you this far?
What reckless odor had betrayed your trust?
In all life's awe and inspiring bliss,
Some kisses deserve a pedestal more than others.
Lips, creamy and succulent, wet with anticipation,
Hungry with tastes and distastes, state and stasis,
Rose-petal lips of a mountain lion's mouth a tiger devours,
Prowling en route, continental crossing,
Borders possible to penetrate seamlessly,
Freedom like stars in the sky,
Somewhere above, a name I had heard before,
I repeat the breathing patterns of my lover,
Heaving chest, brawn on my skin.
I work for days and nights imagining you
In another encounter where my rapture lies,
Thigh up-and-down, loving like birds in flight,
Frightened of what secrets could be revealed
For now, and for then, I long for you until my lips
Are parched, thirsty for the wrong things felt, seen and unseen.
I am all you have to be human.
Eye me. I can see what's inside of you.

Socrates & Plato

For Dr. Nikitopoulos

Socrates—your Plato, here.
Greece & Western civilization, the Parthenon,
Stay idol worshiper,
Nude as beautiful as the invisible shape of Athena
Envying the beauty of man.
Give me Asia Minor
& a battleship sailing the Euphrates
Into the Gulf and around to the Nile,
Bind your destiny to mine wrapped in silk and soaked
In the pleasantry of Asian spices.

Where I am from, dawn is halfway ahead of yours,
But in Lowell, at the exact Eastern time,
You speak of Greek immigrants who forgot their past.
Athena's smell of feta cheese, Gyros & Baklava,
Ambiance songs and dances,
Rocks and cobblestones

Lowell together, teacher & student,
Geography and history, one giant leap, an immigrant at a time—
Racketing sexy looms: bump-it, bump-it, bump-it,
Sounds of ancient bedsprings of New Englanders
Making love shamelessly.
From Ellis Island the poor and wretched seek a new start
Like Yankee daughters who left their dolls
For work, when they should have been playing.

You tell me of changes and similarities,
One in the shoes of the other,
The new replacing the old,
But the new ones repeat experiences the old forgot.

You taught me this much—
When leaving home with nothing, take what you can to survive,
And then root yourself in the new place
Where you can lay the foundation of a home.

Cast away all prejudices, all stones of judgment.
Immigrants or refugees pass through here
Where the Irish dug the canals.
Will I succeed?
I will never forget to look over my shoulder.
You won't be turned into stone, you said.
But wisdom you'll gain.
What life isn't worth a second chance?

American Rodents

Rodents golf-conspiring to take over. Surrounding trees and shrubs listen to them, waiting to see, who, among these rats will take the greatest chunk of their air, water, and land their free-enterprise can buy and sell in a democratic manner. Constitutional power cartwheels across the manicured lawn, down with the white hard ball rolling closer to the designated hole, the target.

A bullseye. Men of power greet each other with caution and formality. Wall Street is good when there's chaos in La Maison Blanche. The national debt rises, and the next generation will pay. Old men close to death forfeit the future for sex and domination. They possess rodent nature to bring yet another plague of hate, interpersonal violence, and war among phalluses. White supremacists are feeling small. The dogs will bark only for attention. They battle for crumbs when the tough is hard to chew. Bitter roots spoil their humanity. They seek the lynching of others to please the cross and a sacrificial lamb to sweeten their teeth. Scarcity and greed make them scavengers on the hunt for glory and fame. Their spotlighted manhood is spitting with lies. They need to learn to speak their mother tongue. They are brutes too vile for Americans' civilized taste. The electoral system put them on that oval chair to mock the presidential rights and privileges constituted by forefathers who understood the nature of rodents, where they live and hide, where they hunt and breed, and where they conspire to become obsolete rulers of the earth, golfing.

First Time

Once I stood in a heated room, quivering while he undressed himself. Undressing me an old man with wrinkles on his face. Never before had I seen a private part so big and alive. Like pulses of a resurrecting heart the Egyptian had mummified and raised from the dead. I froze, shame on my tongue, all curious to squeeze what was throbbing into a full invitation. My heart was beating so that a deaf man could hear it. Closer to him, his callused fingers touched my virgin, unexplored skin—brown glinting into gold, I took his hold, boldly tenderizing myself to be devoured, envious of the tiger telling me to run but I would not. A prey a predator loves, I had prepared myself to be his food. I entered willingly. He didn't force or abduct me. He wasn't a rapist of my innocence, but willingly I approached him, and he approached me, predator to predator, one a bit more dominant than the other.

The night was dark and I had nowhere to go, San Francisco too big to roam, too wild on the street, so I entered and took my chances inside his house, where I had thought all sorts of things, like Ted Bundy's face, pointy nose, red eyes at point blank peered deep into my lungs. Like a shower of dust filling my nostrils, I breathed prayers like rosary beads of a nun as he comforted me with his tongue. The warmth of his saliva on the tip of my nipples. I was engulfed by his flame. I set myself on his fire. His dragon breath power beyond substance as he took me inside, & like a child I squirmed and squealed, I snaked past judgment and shame, I collapsed quickly inside his throat, my knees too weak for right from wrong, from friend or foe, I knew nothing of love or sex. I had seen no one naked. I had not lain with another man old enough to be my grandfather.

It was something never to forget—in a blink, I saw him begging for arousal, as if his kind angel had descended from the sky. He said,

Stay the night, so I did, covering myself up with half of his blanket and dirty white sheets. The next morning, I was grateful to be alive, to discover I had clothes to wear, and socks and shoes to run into the city with other fear and shame. My virginity in the mouth of an old man I didn't or couldn't love. I refused his penetration, but I left with the smell of his breath lingering on my skin, such that I couldn't rub it off in a shower. And since then, I've known that a prey cannot meet another prey. Predator and prey swallow time, they consume each gulf of earth's tongue and fire—paralyze me & make me forget that I can run.

Leave Now

I want the life of a bird,
The free spirit of a wolf,
The task-oriented will of an ant.
I want the strength of a shark.

I want the tears of an elephant,
The joy of a giraffe stretching its neck to pick
The freshest, tender tip of a leaf,
The fluidity of a snake coiling in the grass or water.

I can still reach for the sky in my imagination,
Reaching it by ship or plane,
A metal bird matching my desire for flight.
I don't want to stay in one place.

I need wings.
Wings to carry me over mountains and the oceans.
Wings that span and span beyond modern existence,
A place to live with more time for contemplation.

Life in America is fierce and harsh.
It's suicide. Backaches and pain. Aggression.
My old habits of introversion spur sadness and despair.
Toiling unsatisfied and unfulfilled. There's more out there.

I've had my epiphany.
The light on my shoulders outshines the sun.
My wings are crafted. No need for bird-advice.
My imagined flights take me farther.

Leave now.

Nature's Revulsion

Between two rivers a parallel universe, fish of the same kind swim and play. They circulate the same blood. Dark purple when bled. They have the same sail-like fin, same shape of eyes and color, blue, ringed with black, the kind Saturn doesn't have. Maybe it does, but you can't see it. Everything in the two rivers, the same bedrocks, fresh plankton, and algae. Its composition flows toward the same purpose, toward a larger body of water, far beyond the horizon, they merge into one, but unaware of their different sources with the same genetic copies that carried Earth's blood before the time of Man.

As man claimed the world, he chiseled and cut everything and said parallelism does not exist. He built dams. He dug channels in the rivers for cargo ships. He changed Nature every way to suit himself by leveling mountains, downing the trees, short-cutting the rivers, stopping water flow to make electric power. But the rivers, now, larger, aware of each other, have become stronger and wider. They conspire with the clouds, the sun, and the moon, the spirits of dead trees that man logged in the mountains, and the oceans, animals of land and seas, to overthrow with heat and flood Man's rule over the planet. Death to man! Nature chants.

She Is Time

Rivers on the landscape of her face. Tears mark years that passed.
She may enter the volcanic fire, melting into the ocean of death.

Dark holes of stars, black matter of epochal memories, close up.
Gone are youthful summer blooms of love and passion.

Aging is torture, burning with loneliness.
She sits folding napkins into squares to be stuffed into her socks.

Her life now disconnected blurs. Her sons also aging.
They have become strangers to her familiar environment.

Their names slipped from her arteries.
They move in the house she no longer runs.

The graveyard where she decorated her mother's tomb
Waits for her. And sons will inherit the ritual of remembrance.

Time thinned her skin. It surfaced her veins that bruise easily.
Her hair grays into strands of loose yarn.

Her eyes are dry. No one talks to her, so she talks to herself,
The self that time has stolen, the self that doesn't know itself.

Open your door! Find remembrance in the grave.
She waits for death, not knowing when to go. Blank.

In Her Absence

My sunny arrival met the cordial grief & despair of her sons. An airport mounting with losses just before the Coronavirus—each picking, one variety of apples to another. Pear from nectarines, peaches from plums. Filled baskets in the back of a truck. Seasonal departure & arrival find her older & older. Demented & frail, going sooner or later.

The day she left, gray clouds & fog, misting overcast. The world I had left and returned to is unchanged, from exterior glances, the trees as they were, leafless & cold, covered with snow.
This morning, the woman I expected to find, see, and hear isn't in her usual spot, a mother & a familiar friend. I looked over to her favorite couch, sat at her kitchen table and next to her

favorite chair, with my usual cup of decaffeinated coffee,
Toasting with her cup of tea with milk.
Nothing but empty space & a sense of void
The kind silence whispers of an abandoned nest.
Past private mourning all is gray & opaque. Into small details
Of shared moments—one is never really physically subtracted,
Though life hangs out in all sorts of weather.

The forecast is hotter & hotter. The temperature gets more intense. The passing of a life is freedom beyond this physical boundary or confinement. Out there, yes, but void & empty space. In spacetime, there's no way of knowing how to go, when & where are the questions. A great, great loss. In her absence, her room is full of folded clothes.

Groundhog Day

You seek doors to other dimensions.
Open your rocky blinds. My intentions are clear.
I wish to enter the sky through your corridors beneath earth.
Take away these regrets and sorrow.
Bury them like you would my flesh.
Give me sun when I am alive, take me down
The rain-fed rivers of my ancestors,
And on a raft slide me down a mountain of snow.

I think you know the secrets to shorten distances
Between earth and the universe.
You can do sound travel in your blood.
At the slightest tremble you learned to run, to hide and live quietly.
With your natural claws you can dig.
You can build like a humble architect who makes a stone roof.
You sculpt clay into a colony for breeding a brood of dreamers
And scientists traveling the stars. Travel through wormholes
Into the arms of other galactic inhabitants.

Burrow through salted quartz of mathematical calculations,
Navigating the sea, tunneling in and out of crevices
Invisible to man, far greater than all metaphors.
You can decode the passage of time.
Are there secrets to the whereabouts of stars?
Do you feel a slight change in earth's route around the sun?
What tremors, what fear, what joy do you hear?
What gravitational force to play such grand musical notes,
Such grand scales of life and its miracles?

You feel the temperature and every quake of the ocean bed.
You read the signs of volcanic fire stirred by the sun.

What bread and butter do humans churn?
What star-yearning hearts float here?
What spoken sacred vows star-people left you?
Is there a creator?
Is there an organized purpose to this existence?
Is it by luck or by chance that we arrived here?
Who originated you? Is it water? Is it the sun?

Out the Window

The window is a mirror that isn't simply frontal reflection. Inside, I see shapes and colors hidden from the light. The darkness can reveal something that light can't. Light isn't always a revelation. Day and night are different orders and realms. Each realm is a personality. It can be a Shakespearean king confiding in the witches of time to obtain predictions and secrets of tomorrow. Day, what it reveals, can be half the truth, giving each color a name, each likeness its characteristics, each awakening a new set of tools to describe what's beautiful to behold, what blemishes to disregard.

Without light, night is reduced to black and grayish white, and then all black. In this blackness, there can be pictures of nature at various points of life and death. Rebirths and countless secrets of buried leaves and decomposition, nutrients that feed the earth, beneath snow, seeds in hibernation.

Just as there are myriad of stars in the universe, the window takes in nature's ways during calm or chaos, absorbs its temperature, hot or cold, its moods, the cry of wind or her flurry snowstorm, when spring returns, she conspires to bring birds and the bees to sing and dance. Everywhere, the bees hide, buzz and fly—when spring is done, they travel elsewhere for food—those flowers whose nectar they digest and make love to, and in their tasks, their duties, their services or sacrifices, life is a fleeting moment like that of raindrops, which, once grounded, the earth collects into brooks and streams.

For a moment, I'd sit to mourn their absence, in the cold wind, ground frozen still and all the leafless bent trees, the gestural drawings covering the canvas sky. I see no bees, but other insects, window screen in or out, even in the winter, manage to thrive like the mad loud buzzing fly trapped in warmth trying to commit suicide, in a blindfolded attempt to escape into the freedom of the cold, banging against the wall or the window. I silenced it with the sole of my foot. I would not have done it to bees because they contribute human life. I love their fragile wings, dedication, and speed.

The windows are another set of eyes noticing the passing sun, the gray stillness, and the blanched color of despair. During an illumination, the light inside makes the darkness clear with silhouettes of trees, high at one glorious peak to another, the uneven terrain between earth and sky, pencil lines, shadows of limbs, branches without a single tremor, set for dawn and back to dusk.

I have no other places to go in this quiet gray world. The snow-covered hill. Distant evergreen. The bell rung deep in the forest. No moss or fern in my room. I have prepared my urn for the ashes a person can spread when I'm dead. I see the trees on the shores where I roamed. Men and women had secrets in domes and spires carved into the sky above the strange but familiar sandy sunny shores past the window—where I should run.

The Four Sons

Each year, small increments of change, fragments gone unnoticed are evidence of age, guarded secrets and the unsaid, the unspoken, the silenced decomposing beneath snow. They are shaped and bent to motion, the aches and pain of work. The shafts rusting in neglect. Their hands and feet grow callused. Arms and thighs go haggard with swallowed pride, the lies and truth of endurance and shame, the road to death full of trials and tribulation. Apples and peaches drop and rot. Pears and plums melt into stones that won't seed or grow. The first snow never comes at an exact time of month. It stormed down, and then the sun warmed the ground. The birds left to find fresh flowers. The turkeys don't scratch the snow. Geese above are past fall migration. TV speaks of things far away.

Someone has fallen to illness with surgery due, another flees inner thoughts and fantasies. When young, they had such will to work with little play. Food on the table and a car to drive girls to the movies. By happy invitations, women with a set of instructions, came and went from their lives. Some left them for other men, leaving them scars to resist the desires of the flesh. Here among these fruit trees, one season to the next, I understand life—how slow death can be on a certain day or night when even the will to live can be frightening—and when to open and close my eyes.

The Longing Dagger

To be forced to cut my layers of flesh, veins of eastern blood,
What rivers I had known before you got off a ship
In a foreign suit and tie, shouting at birds,
That handkerchief tucked in your dark pocket to flag me.
What a fool I was to fall into the arms of your foreign vanity!
French perfume choked me in the night.
I would have eaten your tongue, taken your eyes for mine,
Taken out your heart to grill, feasting on your European utterances,
French hissing to the humid, sunny American-Khmer.

Educated in poetic justice, the way of lies,
The economy of flesh-sharing,
The manners of bedding shared desire and the art of masturbation.
You gave me well-disguised germs colonizing your mouth.
The ravishing lips' rouge misled me to dine and wine.
I breathed the crowding scent of your body.
I inhaled the smoke of your Marlboro Lights.
I listened to your snores.
I watched your pink eyelids closing,
And in the dark, I reached to your face with my palm
Wanting you all to myself, your pubis of moss, your balls of a bull,
Monkey hair on your chest, the groin I shaved.

What love earth and sky, half of heaven, the weight of an ocean,
At your gulf's shore, inside a mosquito net, the doubts on your back,
Spinal and spider, inward to a disease growing inside.
You had no courage to face it—shame mapped your roads.
In secrecy, your love for me died, yet I took your cuts and bruises,
Trying to be your friend and lover, but no, a singular despair,
A life dressing up for your French upper class,
The aristocracy of your pale flesh without substance.

Inside you, nothing but emptiness, the longing dagger
Couldn't absorb the blood it bled from one lover to the next.
What a shame to be a disease that pushes others away.
I could have loved you more than I loved myself.

The Man of Class

The man who can return his love for mine
Wears suits and ties to the movies,
Polished black shoes that boast of his arrival.
Here, he's king, the white man wears the crown.

He has a heart of class and money
From years of earning for the locals,
Who serve him and ensure that he will survive.
He, employer from colonial masters, still walks

For the jewels of the poor,
Enameled by their own marks of social security,
Privileges and power, stoic and indifferent,
My love washed in suds and foam from the ocean's tides.

I am no different from the life
Of his servant, without class, though I equaled,
Even surpassed, all his learning and degrees.
For love, I was willing to lose myself,

For his betrayal, French wines, and high fashion
And security, beside the ocean's bed,
Crashing to his waves of arrogance,
Cuddling to fantasies that he would love me as I loved him,

Remembering the details and contour of his face,
The hair he shed that I picked from my pillow.
He had me shouting madly when he told me to leave.
Frozen at his feet, I begged and explained.
Indignant and propelled to curses and exchange of blame,
I denied my own humanity to love the love he can't return.

He never loved me.

I rose from sorrow to a head of light when a new love arrived.
He took my breath, another lie, another mistake when, bereft,
I inhaled the perfume at my door.

In Every Life of a French Man

In Thailand he leaves everything French behind.
Guadalupe a distant island, descending to lamentation at sea.
He traded for the mountain of Mae Taeng, Chiang Mai.
His Thai wife is at his side weathering sun and monsoon rain.
He must learn the language of the spoken, unspoken east,
Relocate and reorient western stars where he can see
Above mountainous terrain, an earthen house on the foot of a hill,
Overlooking his valley and rice fields.

What French life he had is a dinosaur, gone.
His past was buried without a marker.
His Thai wife, with whom he can grow old and share meals,
Masters self-control and sanity—what beauty he sees in her,
She sees in him. Her mountains now his, her valley
And the land of her forefathers she tends beside him.

The French man her convert to Buddhist ways,
A simple life that reduces waste,
With meals harmless to other sentient beings.
She is the east who has lived her husband's west.
Together they travel with few belongings
To lighten the load, no car or mansion.
They bike and live close to the earth.

At dawn the French man looks east for his sun,
Looks up for his star, sharing his heart with his love,
Her long, black hair spilling over his pillow,
Itching his pointy nose. Her eyes beaming black at his shore.
They plow fields in the valley below their hill,
Where all French bitterness passes.
He can breathe free of French wines and cheese at last.

First Rain

The miracle of cleansing rain.
Flashing light lashes at me trembling in the shower.
The giant's roar thunderous and tumultuous.
Downpour takes the ground floor to rivers and streams.
The earth drinks through the grass-roots.
The trees are happy. The seeds sprout.
Life thrives in crevices of concrete and between rocks.
Rain greens, cleans, and redeems.
Rain resurrects shine and sheen.
Everything grows.

Don't Force Me to Beg

The river flows.
Must I be still?
Must I know hunger and thirst?
My jobless state is seeking employment,
But no one has offered me a chance.
I can't prove myself.
This city is big, but I am small.
I am a man without social status.
I stand shorter than the rest.
I know no one.
I have little education.
I live in a temple.
I eat leftovers.
I wish to go where the river
Goes, as part of a body,
Naturally on its course,
Moving instead of idling,
With my brain trafficked
In sadness and sorrow.
Alone in a city, underfed,
Waiting for my fate to improve,
Wishing someone would give
Me a chance for a life that others have.
I want to work and earn money.
I want a home and a family.

Oh, life, don't force me to beg.

PARIS

An Escape Route

A tree canopy shades me.
Mosquitoes want my blood.
A perspiring American, I sit
Pondering how I got this far,
To this very spot under pines and oaks.
I recognize the heat and humidity.
April 17, 1975—in my face as if I can touch it.
On that sweltering Khmer New Year night, I heard a gun.
I sweat profusely as fear rises.
My mother had just had a premonition in her right eye,
An eclipse, veiled, cast-over,
Brushed past her brow.

Where I now hide, an American,
Safe and secure from the scorching sun,
Crickets take me back to the stench of corpses.
No matter how American I've become,
Cambodia's forever my shadow.
Alone with an iced coffee, I inked out a poem
About farming to evade another nightmare.
The August breeze keeps me alert, alive.
My next escape will be the south of France,
Country of *parfum* and lavender,
Into the arms of a dying friend,
Another winter without a New England Christmas.

The Church Bell

It strikes on the clock, every hour, each ring a breath.
I climb to his spare room where I sleep, thinking of us
Waging peace within shared history, however brief.
Short as our time was, we hadn't thought of separation,
When, during a period of youthful air, death left us alone.
We lived like happy fliers, needing no nest,
Like children on a merry-go-round, in a circus,
Where clowns gave us glad frights from within.

His breath is now mine, one falling, the other catching up,
Staccato tunes mine after his, mine lagging, skipping a few beats.
I hear the sound of the oncoming train of my past,
My breath in and out of his timeline, far from his celebrations,
His body of joy, his lips making notes while he plays the piano.
More and more distant and inaudible, my breath in shadows,
Running from the past, drifting, a loner aiming for a dead star.

In what paradise can I breathe the bird songs?
My breath synced with his, a narrower inflection,
I thought of what could have been, what we could have shared,
What adventures on the backs of elephants, on the wings of birds,
What flesh lions can hunt, what Sahara to sink our flags in,
What love between comrades to cross foreign borders?

This ding, a chime so fatal now that he's on the brink,
The dying unconsciousness of everything he had lived.
We are at the end, he is ending, leaving me to my lonely end,
Without a friend like I had been his.
Each passing hour, the idea of a miraculous cure,
Being saved by the bell,
Feels more like a dream

In which Lazarus returns to glorious life,
And we laugh again about our silly desires for prowling men,
All on the lookout for death when we had life.

I know why he's dying. I'm here to play Jesus.

An Elephant, He Went an Ant

An elephant, he went an ant—
Tiny puff scurrying into the grass and weeds of his garden.
He wasn't too old, but he wasn't young enough to resist dying.
Lymphoma spread, an organ at a time. The kidneys went, then lungs,
The heart the last stand, pumping vital blood full of sex and fun.

Always on the road, between homes, each season a continent,
Across the Atlantic or the Pacific, in bars and restaurants,
He drank like a seal swallowing the sea, looking for company,
Talking sex and wet dreams since puberty,
Before the time of AIDS, even past its first wave of death.

Now at home December whispers chilled gossip at his door.
A short walk between stone walls on cobblestoned paths.
Golden sun lit the tiled brick roof of his neighbors.
Window mountain view the size of a large Van Gogh.
His time is recorded on the rocks and stones in this village.

With an inheritance, he modernized his summer home
Running water, books, and lights. Schumann on a piano near him.
I woke to his slightest groan of pain—in the dim light,
He lay on an adjustable bed, stationery in discomfort,
Thin face, jaws and nose, like dying Jesus on the cross

Waiting to be received by his holy father,
Closing his eyes when I came down.
His face shone from the ceiling light.
I had no words, no wisdom, just silence, my hands felt his face,
Touching loose hair while invitations rose from medieval walls.

Reincarnate across time and space.
Free yourself from earthly flesh.
Travel across the stars to a more
Lustrous friend out there than I can ever be.

Come inside the grass, said the ant.

The Body

Two undertakers arrived, but it took only one to discard the body. A roll-over transfer into a bag, zipped up like a dead soldier being sent home from a foreign war. Quickly into a van and away to the morgue, where a mortician would prepare him for cremation, wondering about a life he had lived. Though life had fled, this body had had a life before. The mortician wouldn't know him like I knew him—a lover, not a fighter. Love was what killed him. He needed a lot of it, so he went looking for it wherever he could. Often, just for mere physical interaction, insertion and exertion of the body. He rarely discussed with anyone what he lacked—only what he had: privileges and money to buy sex. There was some love in the mix. A full moon was love. Andromeda was love. So was Orion. He would point to them while holding someone's hand. Look, he said, How beautiful it is. Out there light years away. Every sparkle is a sun. How infinite the universe seemed. How small his life was. Though he felt big and smart, he fell hard for every man below him.

His dollars had poor boys loosen their clothes, whispering, "Me love you long time." The ones he loved most were given a European tour de force. London. Paris. The Amsterdam flats and canals, culture and museums, the tulips, Anne Frank's Holocaust, architectural lessons. The Gothic of a Parisian cathedral, the gargoyles on guard, deflecting away evil on the rooftop, out in the rain, weathering down. As he got older, his body sagged and his breasts loosened. The boys he loved became the gargoyles of his end. They spread for him to go inside, knowing their blood could have been spoiled and tainted by other older men in their past. He went anyway, in and out, often in low-lit rooms, from hotel to his private abode, the scent of semen and a condom breaking brought the undertaker to his house. The body now has bones of pale flesh.

A body, during hours of pitch darkness, worked itself to the final end. A body, when touched, dented like clay. White skin went pork, so empty of breath. The blood inside went purple and still. He swelled into liquid inside a stagnant well. All the rivers in his veins stopped running their courses as the oxygen fell lower. He didn't believe in God, so I couldn't pray or read him a verse from the Bible. A homo is always an outcast of Eden. He was too proud to take rejection, so he brought even God to His knees. It was between him and the devil, so the hell with heaven.

Take away the body!

Parisian Streets

Je suis perdu. A wanderer, full of angst, as private and internal as a soliloquy. To God, questions without answers—the why and how—the what? What insanity to fuel such greatness in man? What grand designs had God inspired? Paris is gigantic and bold, a breathless sojourn, I can't even grasp my own existence. I am belittled by it all, even at the highest peak of heaven, I find hell, reaching for the stars hidden behind winter's gray sky. I walked a nomad's life, wishing to set up a tent when tired of the incomprehensible, all too good to be true, as truth being taken hostage by someone else's prophecy of self-made narrative, born from original sins.

I see Jesus with his thorny crown wreath, half the sacrifice his body to man, his blood as the River Seine, the nails that bled him from the cross are now pain in my eyes, my head and my sore feet, as I wander, I look without knowing what I am looking for, but I look and look, until my eyes are strained, and my head anxious from too many connecting nerves and electrodes trying to translate what I see into three different languages, with my maternal one incapable of naming even the concept of a museum or a cobblestone street, full of people drinking coffee in tiny cups outside in January.

There had been days when I crossed Pont Neuf, I thought of cleaning Jesus' feet, if he would let me, to heal his nail wounds with my own tears because I love him that much. He had saved my urge to drown with the sound of a church bell from the belfry of St. Michel, where I found angels no one had seen, as if I was given special power to see the dead. They don't actually have wings as they have been imagined, but fins to save people from suicide. I thought of jumping to test their hearts, whether I would be the one they would care to save. I get so lonely that their company was a perfect wish to be granted—in death and into their arms, I can gain fins for the River Seine and her grief. All Parisian streets collapse over me like a catacomb once intended for the beheaded. I plead to be saved, oh, Savior, angel Gabriel, give me the fins to snorkel across time so I can reclaim my throne.

The Metro

It lives with me, this underground map—when far away, I can visualize this crying train, braking on the tracks, squealing slowly to a stop, doors opening to exhale and inhale, the puffing of fatigue French R: RER, *respirer, respect et train!* Internal whispers, crowded and overcrowding heads of any color, humanity moving, en masse, route en route, rasping sounds, breathless at the end of a marathon racing for love, and for life—anything to fill the emptiness and loneliness inside.

Silence of passing eyes is replaced by the train in its climax of speed and from speed to brake, embracing its track ever so tightly, ever so urgently, fearful of derailing passengers inside, holding on to dear life, neck to neck with someone they wish to love or to hate, what pleasure the body will give for a night of anonymous sex. Tenderness comes when the train opens to fresh air, passengers in and out like a trap to and from places and destinations, arrival and departure from someone or something, the singers offer their off-key songs, sometimes an orchestra inside the tunnel, where my heart is heard inside my head, hoping for the one I had lost in the past, if only he would reappear, I would follow him to the end of the earth. I would be willing to give him all my breaths in his mother tongue. *Bonjour. Je veux être avec toi.*

Out by the river, without direct sunlight, it's dark as the blood in my body. The river flows as do rivers in my body, full of tunnels and train tracks of veins the size of a single strand of hair, from which organs make lakes and oceans, dark as oil even in the light, the night shimmers gold glistening on water, and the chill of night caresses erupting fire inside. What tears to shed alone in a foreign city where I walk miles? If only I could travel in my own lit veins, what would I see? Is it the same landscape as this city?

The rivers cut through, and the organs are containers and wells like human sewage and water tunnels, veins where blood flows like water downstream upstream, rain pulling down the sky, hell dams the current, every man dies but each life is an engineering feat, a symbolic extraordinary exterior that flows out of his internal beauty, greed, hunger, and thirst, his fear, all of which protect him from harsh elements of nature—he dresses and undresses his body, before, during, or with earth's wind, fire, and water, rising beyond his gift to fashion himself in the image of God. He shines light to see what's inside his own darkness.

The Economy of Longing

Shops entered, shops exited,
Longings & receipts in bags,
Plastic & paper to be discarded after one use,
Something to hold,
Something to grab,
Adornment to please,
Flowers in bloom forever,
The glitter and shine of life,
The loneliness for the old,
The never felt and never seen,
Breaking into borders and crossings,
Self-invited thief with nothing to steal,
This empty touch,
These secrets veiled from the public,
Approachable, hung guilt-free,
What subsistence to wander aimless,
Floundering in the dark,
Inside the cavities of time,
Stock & economic court & army,
But baffled violence for the rules of law
Where all yearnings are jailed from view,
What these longings do to solitary contemplation
Bitter at the act of persuasion
Corrupted and cheated of breath,
Hard at work toward restoration & free movement
Without any conforming relational ties
To blind my eyes from seeing my own truth,
Selling if I have to, my own longing for a bag
Of potato chips.

Paris, I can eat you up.

EPILOGUE

THE WAY   I WANT
TO REMEMBER
MY   CAMBODIA

I want to remember how I was free to run in the field
eyeing the sky—my handmade kite flying high,
loving the wind, loving the clear white cloud.

I want to remember how I was free to run in the sun,
free to own and roam the fields, free to walk and sing
to myself or to the God of the hills full of trees, to green
rice paddies, to the pond's pink lotus and muddy swamp,
to the crystal tune of an overflowing river, to the rainbow
of my felicity and the wild dogs' red mating call.

I want to feel the flirtatious air caressing my naked body
in childhood innocence wrapped in the arms of my brothers.

I want to remember the shrilling cry of crickets hidden
under broken planks, the way I went earring for them
in the mist of dawn to capture them in my jar, my chase
after dragonflies, my slingshot pebbles passing birds, and how
I spent day after day fishing, netting grasshoppers in the sun,
its burning heat, and the times I searched for beetles in
cow manure while herding cattle and water buffalo.

I recall my mother's cooking fire, her salted-fish grilled
on burning charcoal, the smell of her boiling stew, her
sharp knife drumming the cutting board. In her outdoor
kitchen, the smoke of her art hissed out of her wok, moving
into the air like a cobra shedding its skin on our fence.

I want to feel my dark Cambodian skin crack from playing
with earth, to see my boyish brown eyes staring at green
bamboo, to feel myself leaning to soak in the fragrant
yellow-flowered hills. I want the serenity of blue ponds
and the white river of childhood, and to feel
the wind wiping away the dew on my body.

I want my peasant home, to still be in that village among
the surviving people on that laboring earth where I was born.

My Cambodia, tell me again the stories of how the old
ghosts take possession of human souls, how monsters
shape the art of death. I want to hear how the Goddesses
turn what is ugly into something beautiful.
Make me part of that secret. Let me dance in your sun.

Acknowledgements

A huge thank you to the editors of the publications in which some of these poems first appeared, sometimes in earlier versions: *Children of the Killing Fields: Memoirs of Survivors, Consequence Magazine, The Merrimack Literary Review, The Bridge Review: Merrimack Valley Culture (www), Where the Road Begins, RichardHowe.com, History as It Happens: Citizen Bloggers in Lowell, Mass.,* and *Atlantic Currents: Connecting Cork and Lowell.*

This book would not be possible without Loom Press—Paul Marion, Rosemary Noon and Joseph Marion. Thank you for believing in this manuscript and publishing it the traditional way when others turned their backs. Thank you to Ken and the Nicewicz family for allowing me to live and work on their fruit, vegetable, and flower farm in Bolton, Massachusetts, and for embracing me as a family member. I wrote and painted in my spare time or during the winter months when I am not traveling. Being on a small family farm provides peace in the midst of Nature.

To all the teachers in my life: I would not have made it this far without your kindness and belief in my potential. Almost magically, you appeared and showed me the way out of darkness and into light—the path to a life worth living is through knowledge and literature. Thank you, Mrs. Brunot, Mr. Doyle, Mrs. Climp, and Mr. Allen, who made the Elizabethan period come alive. And I am most grateful to Dr. Charles Nikitopoulos, Dr. Nik, who helped me earn a master's degree in community social psychology at the University of Massachusetts in Lowell. My biggest fan, he always attended my readings and encouraged me as a friend, a teacher, and a father. The poem "Socrates and Plato" is about our relationship. Dr. Linda Silka and her husband, Larry, supported my education and research financially. Elizabeth Ross Johnson contributed to my Southeast Asian languages studies at the University of Wisconsin, Madison. And Rick Sawyer, who has passed away, paid for my first writing workshop that was taught by the poet Martin Espada.

Friends, near and far, you are in my heart. Your support helps me grow stronger as a human being and as a writer, and to find a way to illuminate our shared experiences as our paths cross, whether in sadness or joy. Praise to Cambodia, my family there, and to her resilient and hopeful people, and to the United States of America, a country without which I would not be writing all this.

About
the Author

Chath pierSath was born in Battambang, Cambodia in 1970, survived the Khmer Rouge genocide, and left the country as a refugee, finally settling as a boy in Denver, Colorado. He earned a bachelor's degree in International Service and Development from World College West/New College of California in San Francisco. He returned to Cambodia in 1994 to volunteer in the human rights field with the Cambodian American National Development Organization and later worked in youth education programs in Lowell, Massachusetts, where he earned a master's degree in community social psychology at UMass Lowell. The author of two collections of poetry, *After* and *This Body Mystery*, and a children's book, *Sinat and the Instrument of the Heart*, his writing has also appeared in various publications. Known internationally as a visual artist, he has shown his paintings in Asia, Europe, and North America. He lives and works on a family farm that grows fruits, vegetables, and flowers in Bolton in the Nashoba Valley of central Massachusetts.